A PARCEL OF

'Does Lt. Wilberforce pay you compliments?'
Edward asked.

'About my riding do you mean? He could
scarcely compliment me on my looks!'
Harriet shot him a droll glance. 'Though he once
said I had a determined chin!'

'Obstinate is the word for it,' Edward said.
'And I fear that it may get you into trouble . . .'

A Parcel of Land

Mary Ann Gibbs

CORONET BOOKS
Hodder and Stoughton

Copyright © Mary Ann Gibbs, 1969

Published by arrangement with the author and the author's
agents, John Cushman Associates, Inc.

First published by Beagle Books Inc., New York, 1973

Coronet Edition, 1976

_____

Printed and bound in Great Britain for
Coronet Books, Hodder and Stoughton, London,
by Richard Clay (The Chaucer Press), Ltd,
Bungay, Suffolk

ISBN 0 340 20514 8

1

Two small boys were fighting each other on the opposite side of the street, while two others pressed their noses to the window of the baker's shop where a tempting display of pies were to be seen. Mrs. Tycherley wondered why it was that the small boys in Gale Street appeared to have but two thoughts in their minds: to fight each other, or to stare at food.

All four were indescribably dirty and ragged, their feet bare, their faces sharp under the grime, and Gale Street itself was not much better, being situated in a neighbourhood that had come down in the world. Mrs. Tycherley looked out of the grimy window on the parlour front of Number Thirty Seven and regretted her pretty house in Tunbridge Wells, and supposed that the world might say —if it could be so unkind—that she and Harriet had seen better days too.

Except for the doctor's house at the more select end, the baker's shop in the middle, and the coffee-house on the far corner, Gale Street was given up to the letting of lodgings, mostly to ladies and gentlemen in the acting profession. Number Thirty Seven was small and dingy, and the two rooms that Mrs. Tycherley rented there, though grandly called the parlour front, showed signs that former tenants had treated them with scant respect.

Their landlady, Mrs. Slatterly, had a penetrating voice and a habit of saying 'Can't 'ear you, mum,' without waiting for Mrs. Tycherley to conclude any small requests she might feel impelled to make. And they were very small requests, not only because the widow's means were slender, but because she was afraid of giving trouble, and especially to Mrs. Slatterly of whom she was quite terrified.

She wished she could open the window and throw down a penny to the small boys at the baker's window, so that they could run into the shop and buy one of the loaves there, as she used to do at Tunbridge Wells with the milk-woman's little daughter. Mrs. Adams had been a fine, good-looking woman, and every morning when she brought the pails of milk swinging from the wooden yoke across her shoulders, the child had come with her, and Mrs. Tycherley had often put a penny into her hand. She had been taught to curtsey so prettily, and though her clothes were shabby they were neatly darned and patched, and her little face was as fresh and sweet as the milk in her mother's pails.

Mrs. Tycherley, being one of the kindest souls on earth, did not like to see children as thin and famished as these London children, though Mrs. Slatterly assured her that they did it on purpose and were that way because they liked it, and if any of them dared to approach her steps she would rush out, brandishing a broom and threatening that she would have them taken up, though where they were to be taken up to Mrs. Tycherley never discovered. And though she felt thankful that her husband had possessed a kind brother, who had not only provided Captain Alfred Tycherley's widow and daughter with enough money for their support but had exerted himself as well to find lodgings for them, what with Mrs. Slatterly's deafness, and the habit their fire had of languishing through lack of fuel, and the noise in the street under their windows, sometimes she was afraid that she did not feel as grateful as she should.

A trio of musicians had now joined the children below, three seedy-looking men sawing away on fiddles and seeming to play any tune that came into their heads, regardless of what their companions were doing, and as if this were not enough a filthy Italian boy began to grind out music from a dilapidated piano-organ several doors up on the other side of the street.

Mrs. Tycherley had half-opened the window to throw down her penny to the children, but she hastily closed it again, and her thoughts returned to the letter that had arrived for Harriet the day before. Mrs. Slatterly's maid-servant had brought it with her from the Post Office with two letters that looked suspiciously like bills for the young gentleman on the second floor back. Mrs. Slatterly liked to keep an eye on her lodgers' correspondence, especially when they were in the acting profession.

Mrs. Tycherley was sorry for the young man, guessing that he scarcely ever indulged in a square meal in spite of his brightly coloured waistcoats and exquisitely tied, grubby, cravats. Whenever he saw Harriet he would bow and remark what a lovely day it had been, but Harriet had that effect on young men, although nobody could call her a beautiful girl. She was not in fact even pretty, her mouth being wide, her nose snub, and her figure small, plump and insignificant.

But whether it was the colour of her hazel eyes, more often green than brown and sometimes a golden blend of both, or whether it was the sweetness of her wide smile, and her eighteen-year-old air of trust and innocence, it remained an indisputable fact that you would not think that any young men who spoke to her had ever experienced a wet day in their lives. And indeed, Mrs. Tycherley thought wistfully, looking back to those dear, departed days at Tunbridge Wells, most of the days there *had* been sunny and warm—an eternal summer in fact, because she could not remember any others even in the middle of winter. Whereas since they had lived in Gale Street they had only seen the sun through a pall of fog and smoke.

Harriet's letter had come from a lawyer's office in Lincoln's Inn, stating that Mr. Theodore Snuff, of Snuff, Banks and Snuff, Attorneys-at-law and Commissioners for Oaths, hoped to call on Miss Harriet Tycherley that morning on a matter of business.

'Business, Harriet, my love!' Mrs. Tycherley, who had a naturally optimistic nature and could never be in the dumps for long, read the letter that her beloved stepdaughter handed to her, and pursed her lips and nodded her head knowingly. 'This can only mean that somebody has left you some money! I am sure of it!'

'I wish I could be as sure, Mamma!' Harriet made a small grimace. 'But there is nobody in the world who would do such a thing. It is far more likely to be another debt that Papa thought he had settled and had not. His memory over some things was very bad indeed, you know.' She did not like to think what her poor uncle would do if he were forced to settle any more of his brother's debts.

Mrs. Tycherley gave a sigh of regret for her departed Alfred. He had not only failed to remember to leave a penny for his widow and his daughter, but he had omitted to pay the rent of the charming little house in Tunbridge Wells where Mrs. Tycherley had lived so happily for a number of years after the death of her first husband, and into which Captain Tycherley had moved with Harriet only four years ago. Although their landlord had begged them to think nothing of it, knowing how they had been situated, they could not blame him for hinting as soon as he felt it to be decently possible after the gallant Captain's funeral, that he would be grateful if they could find other accommodation.

She glanced at the little travelling clock on the mantelshelf—one of her few remaining treasures—and saw that the lawyer was just about due, and as Harriet opened the door and joined her, Mrs. Tycherley studied her appearance with a little anxiety. The mend in her dress did not show, though if the man thought they could pay poor dear Alfred's debts it might be as well if it did. And even if Harriet was not pretty, the London fogs had failed to dim her smile or take the sparkle out of her eyes.

Outside the small boys had taken themselves off to the coffee-house, to press their noses afresh to its windows and to beg for pennies from the customers as they went in and out. The piano-organ had moved away, and so had the three violinists, and for a fleeting second there was peace in Gale Street.

'I have often wished,' said Harriet wistfully, 'that ladies could frequent coffee-houses.'

'My dearest Harriet! What ever makes you wish such an extraordinary thing?'

'Because coffee-houses look so cosy and comfortable, Mamma!' Harriet shot an amused glance at her Mamma's shocked face. 'Every time we pass that one on the corner and I catch a glimpse of the gentlemen sitting there by a lovely fire, sipping their coffee and reading the papers, I wish I could join them. We cannot afford even one newspaper in a week, and I'm sure we would not know if the King were dead, or France had declared war on us and sunk all our ships.'

'If anything as frightful as that had happened, my love, I am sure I would not wish to know about it,' said Mrs. Tycherley decidedly. 'And in any case Mrs. Slatterly would tell us. She always knows all the horrid things that are going on.'

'From the time I can remember to the time when I was fourteen and Papa met you,' Harriet went on dreamily, 'he used to leave me alone in our lodgings while he went to his favourite coffee-house in Holborn. There were no less than nine newspapers for him to read there, and twenty-four magazines every month, besides four quarterly reviews, and all he had to do was to order a cup of coffee, for which he paid three ha'pence, and he could sit there and read to his heart's content.'

9

'Well, there are coffee-houses and coffee-houses, I suppose,' conceded Mrs. Tycherley doubtfully. 'Some of them are very respectable places, I daresay. I do not think they sell spirits there.'

'No, only coffee ... and tea, of course. But that is more expensive. At the Holborn coffee-house there were three rooms, one for hackney coachmen and post lads from Regent Street, and mechanics of all classes, you know, and one for managing clerks and people of that sort, and the third for gentlemen like Papa. He met foreign couriers there sometimes, and then there were gentlemen who lived in the neighbourhood—solicitors and their clients—all highly respectable.'

'But my dearest, the journals supplied to gentlemen in coffee-houses would scarcely be the sort that would interest a lady. I cannot imagine a ladies' journal in such a place.'

'No, I suppose not, but I still think that a penny loaf and a cup of coffee beside a nice bright fire would be preferable to the dishes Mrs. Slatterly serves up to us, and that ... that smoky horror of a grate to sit by.' She glanced out of the window and saw that the street urchins had left the coffee-house and were tearing off after other prey—a gentleman's carriage that had turned in at the top of the street.

As it proceeded down Gale Street, followed by the urchins and another band of musicians, in which a flute was played piercingly out of tune, Mrs. Tycherley and Harriet saw that the coachman on its box was examining the numbers on the doors with an expression of disgust, as if scarcely considering it possible that he could be expected to demean himself by stopping at one of them. He slowed down however as he approached Number Thirty Seven, and Mrs. Tycherley said she felt one of her palpitations coming on.

'Oh no, Mamma, dearest!' cried Harriet. 'You must not

have a palpitation now. I will allow you one after Mr. Snuff has gone ... or perhaps a spasm or two ... But not now!' She found Mrs. Tycherley's smelling bottle and put it quickly into her hand.

'Thank you, my love. I think it is going off,' said Mrs. Tycherley, looking as if she might go off too at any moment. 'Look out of the window and see if he has stopped here.'

Harriet looked, and was able to say that he had. Her calm tone gave no hint of the excitement she was feeling as she watched Mr. Snuff alight from his carriage. From experience she felt she dare not expect anything pleasant to come from the lawyer's visit, but she could not suppress a faint hope that it would.

The lawyer waved the children out of his path with his cane, and they began to shout abuse at the coachman instead, asking who he thought he was, stuck up there with his hat on his head, and would it come off if it was pushed? And much more in the same vein, to his indignation. He threatened them with his whip until they retired to a safe distance, and did the same with the musicians, whose flute frightened the horses.

Mrs Slatterly, who did not seem so hard of hearing that morning, led Mr. Snuff up the dark, winding stairs to the parlour front, and having ushered him in and shut the door, settled herself on the stairs outside the room to hear what was going on, and would no doubt have remained there had not her small maid-servant, in an effort to catch a glimpse of the coachman through the area window, dropped a soup tureen with a crash that reverberated through the house.

Mrs. Slatterly descended like a thunderbolt from the heavens, while Mrs. Tycherley and her step-daughter greeted the lawyer with a well-bred composure that showed not the least awareness of their surroundings, or their landlady's language, or the noisy street in which they lived.

Mr. Snuff bowed, his quick eyes everywhere, on their faces, their dresses and the room that served them for dining-room and drawing-room. He was a little dried-up man, who looked as if he could never have been young but must have been born middle-aged, and he was dressed in a dark brown coat and breeches, his sparse hair hugging the cravat at the back of his neck. He said in a dry little voice, 'Miss Tycherley? Miss Harriet Tycherley?'

Harriet dropped a curtsey. 'I am Harriet Tycherley,' she said. 'And this is my Mamma.'

He directed Mrs. Tycherley the fraction of a bow, indicating that his business was not with her but her step-daughter, and Mrs. Tycherley responded by waving her smelling bottle at him with a feeble smile. Harriet offered him a chair, and he sat down at the table in the window, laying a roll of important looking documents upon it, and having found his spectacles and placed them on his nose, he regarded her over them sternly.

'You are the daughter of the late Captain Alfred Tycherley of the Fourth Dragoons I believe?' he pursued, making sure of his facts before going any further.

'My dear husband fought with the Duke of Wellington at Waterloo,' said Mrs. Tycherley, recovering with unexpected swiftness. 'But I believe he sold his commission many years ago—his health would not allow him to continue in the regiment.'

'I am afraid that any funds my father may have had were exhausted by the time he died,' said Harriet, speaking with a quiet dignity that impressed Mr. Snuff. 'My uncle, who has a family of his own to consider, has already paid more of Papa's debts than we had any right to expect. I am very sorry, sir, if there are more to be met, but my father was not at all good in business matters.'

'But I have not come to demand money from you, my dear young lady,' said Mr. Snuff, a slight warmth creeping into his manner. 'On the contrary I have come to tell you that you have been left some property.'

'Property!' echoed Harriet, while her Mamma jumped up and embraced her.

'I knew it!' she cried. 'Did I not tell you that Mr. Snuff was bringing us good news?'

'Pray control yourself, dearest! You'll bring on a spasm, you know you will!' Harriet pushed her Mamma gently back into her chair and began fanning her with the end of her shawl, while she waited for what else Mr. Snuff had to say.

'Your mother was a lady by the name of Beauregard, I believe,' he said. 'The daughter and only child of the late Sir Robert Beauregard, of Beauregard Manor in the county of Sussex?'

'To be sure my husband's first wife—Harriet's mother —*was* a Beauregard!' cried Mrs. Tycherley, waving the shawl end away. 'She married him against her father's wishes—in fact, they eloped to Gretna Green—so romantic, Harriet, my love! I have often told you how much I envied her! Both my marriages were so humdrum—just a ceremony early in the morning at the local church followed by a simple wedding breakfast. Nothing out of the ordinary . . . But to elope with a handsome young soldier, as my dear Alfred was then, to Gretna Green! What girl would not have given her eyes for such a chance!'

'My grandfather never forgave my mother,' Harriet said when she had allowed her Mamma's exuberance to die down a little, 'and he cut her off without a shilling . . . In fact, he never saw her again.'

'Your grandfather is dead, Miss Tycherley,' said Mr. Snuff.

'And the dear old gentleman experienced a change of heart at the last, and you have come to tell us so!' cried Harriet's Mamma, moist-eyed at the thought of it.

'I am afraid I know nothing about the late Sir Robert

Beauregard's change of heart, madam,' said Mr. Snuff, very drily indeed. 'When he died some years ago it was found that he had left all his property to a distant cousin, Walter Beauregard, who was, I am afraid, rather a wild and dissolute young man, and last February he had an accident—in short, he was found drowned. Everyone thought he would have left the estate to his cousin, Mr. Edward Beauregard, who had been his friend for many years, but he had quarrelled with him as with many others, and he made a fresh will less than six months ago, leaving all he had to his only female cousin—yourself, Miss Harriet.'

He glanced at her over his spectacles and she gave him her wide, enchanting smile, and he went on rather quickly: 'The property is not a large one, and it is considerably impoverished—in fact, it is heavily in debt.'

Harriet's smile deepened: there was little he could tell her about debts that she did not know already.

'You have the Manor House,' he said reprovingly, because it was after all nothing to smile about. 'And you have the land, let out to farmers, but it will bring you in an income of no more, I fear, than six hundred pounds a year.'

2

Harriet wondered if Mr. Snuff knew what a great deal of money six hundred pounds a year represented to Mrs. Tycherley and herself, and she felt nothing but gratitude to her distant cousin Walter, dissolute though he may have been, for having so conveniently quarrelled with Edward Beauregard and left her the property instead.

'I strongly advise you to sell the estate as soon as possible, Miss Tycherley,' went on Mr. Snuff. 'There will be no difficulty about disposing of it, as there are two most excellent prospective buyers in the market for it at the moment. Mr. Sodon, who purchased the Buldrayling estates when old Lord Buldrayling died without an heir more than fifteen years ago, made several offers to Mr. Walter before his death. The Buldrayling estates form the western boundary of your property. And if on the other hand Mr. Sodon does not feel justified in proceeding with his former offer, then I have no doubt that the Marquis of Merrington, whose estates border Beauregard on the east side, will purchase it from you. There are rumours in the neighbourhood—which appear to be well-founded —that Mr. Sodon's eldest daughter, Miss Julia Sodon, may soon become engaged to be married to Viscount Crowley, the Marquis's eldest son, and it is therefore to the interest of both families that the Beauregard land should weld the estates together instead of dividing them as it does now. Mr. Sodon has no son, only five daughters.'

'Indeed?' Harriet regarded him thoughtfully. 'If the Beauregard property is so impoverished, as you said just now, Mr. Snuff, why did not my cousin Walter sell to either Mr. Sodon or the Marquis?'

'Mr. Walter had other ideas for his property.' The lawyer smiled stiffly. 'I believe he wished to marry Miss Julia himself at one time, and indeed presented himself at Buldrayling as a suitor for her hand.' He did not add that Mr. Sodon had threatened Walter Beauregard with a shot-gun if he ever approached Buldrayling again, and continued, 'Mr. Sodon is a banker, and as his eldest daughter will have one hundred thousand pounds on the day she marries, her father is naturally anxious that she should marry into the aristocracy.'

'Let us hope that she will succeed then,' said Harriet almost as drily as Mr. Snuff himself. He hastily untied the tape from one of the documents on the table and spread it out for her to see. 'This is the plan of the Beauregard estate,' he told her. 'Let me show it to you.'

She came to the table and bent over it, examining it carefully. The plan appeared to be of three estates, although only a small part of each of the Beauregard neighbours was shown. The Buldrayling land was coloured buff, the Merrington blue, while between them a small, wedge-shaped piece of grey ran up into the hills towards the turnpike and down into the valley, widening out to include the Manor House, the village of Beauregard, the river with the surrounding meadows, and the estuary that joined the sea between the two headlands.

'This,' said Mr. Snuff, indicating the buff-coloured piece, 'is the Buldrayling estate, and here,' with a finger on the blue, 'is the estate of the Marquis. Both run into many thousands of acres. And here, in between them, is your late cousin's property, now yours, consisting of barely six hundred acres.'

He had forgotten—or perhaps he did not know—that he was talking to a young woman who had lived in lodgings for the first fourteen years of her life, and had only known a home when she had been made welcome in the house of her father's second wife in Tunbridge Wells.

It was there that she had first learned an enjoyment for reading, both in the Circulating Library and from the bookshelves in Mrs. Tycherley's breakfast-room, where romantic novels were more numerous than serious works. On this light fare had Harriet's dreams been fed, until by the time they had to leave Tunbridge Wells for Gale Street, penniless heirs who inherited vast estates had become commonplace.

If her estate, so unexpected and so welcome, was not to be compared with that inherited by Wilfred Penderville in *The Secret of the Pendervilles*, at least her demands were not large either. Here was a house that had been her mother's home and there she could take her dear Mamma, restoring to her the charming social life of which Captain Tycherley's extravagance had robbed her.

'Six hundred acres,' she said slowly, 'may not seem very much to the two gentlemen who appear to wish to buy Beauregard, but I think I would like to visit the Manor before I decide what to do with it.' Her eyes met the lawyer's steadily. 'You see, I might want to live there.'

Mr. Snuff was plainly horrified. 'Oh, but my dear young lady, you could not do that!' he cried.

'Why not?' asked Harriet, interested.

'Well' ... He pursed his lips. 'It is scarcely habitable. The roof leaks, and some of the floors are rotten, and the situation is far too isolated for two ladies to reside there in any safety with such few servants as remain. You would not like it at all.' As she did not reply he hurried on, 'His lordship's man of business has assured me that the Marquis will not be niggardly, if Mr. Sodon does not make a further offer for the land. He is willing to pay twenty pounds an acre which will bring you in a fortune of twelve thousand pounds—one I fancy that any young lady might feel to be a comfortable sum.'

'Twelve thousand pounds!' Mrs. Tycherley clasped her hands ecstatically, her thoughts flying to dear Tunbridge Wells. With such a sum they would be able to buy a charming house like the one where she had lived so happily for such a number of years, with a garden and a stable for a pony and a small chaise. Three maids, and a groom and a gardener would be all that they would need in such an establishment, and she saw herself entertaining her friends again and being entertained by them in return, with the delightful little card parties they had all enjoyed so much, and balls at the dear old Assembly Rooms for Harriet. It was a charming picture, taking her far beyond Mrs. Slatterly's horrid lodgings.

'I think I had better read you Mr. Walter's will,' said

Mr. Snuff, 'while you turn it over in your mind. It is not a very lengthy document.'

He cleared his throat and taking a sheet of paper from the table, began to read, not without some difficulty because there were many blotches to negotiate as well as deplorable spelling. Neither of the ladies paid him a great deal of attention. Mrs. Tycherley's thoughts were still in Tunbridge Wells, and had by this time moved on to the delights of choosing new drawing-room furniture—all hers having been sold to pay their debts—and a carpet for the breakfast parlour, while Harriet's were engaged in picturing an old and no doubt beautiful Manor House, in the midst of splendid gardens full of old-fashioned flowers enclosed by yew hedges, with a river running through the grounds and a view of the sea from the windows.

Into these dreams a phrase or two entered from Mr. Walter Beauregard's will, a curiously worded document, as if the maker of it had not been in the full possession of his faculties at the time and fancied it might sound better if he put in a few bits of what he had termed 'legal jargon'. The words 'this parcel of land known as Beauregard' and 'the demesne and dwelling house known as Beauregard Manor' caught her attention but momentarily however and she waited impatiently until the lawyer had done. Then she asked what the Marquis would do with the Manor House if she should consent to selling it to him.

'Oh, it will be pulled down,' said Mr. Snuff, smiling and gathering his papers together.

'And the gardens and the river?'

'I expect they will be incorporated in the landscape. His lordship is very interested in landscapes. He has done a great deal in that way on some of his other estates.'

'Why, how many has he then?'

'Five altogether,' said Mr. Snuff.

'And yet he wants my little "parcel of land" as well!'

Harriet was puzzled by the workings of the Marquis's mind.

'Mind you,' said the lawyer comfortingly, 'we have not had any serious discussion on the subject as yet. His lordship's man of business, Mr. Quintilian Sprigg, only recently broached the matter to me again, when the details of your cousin's will were known, while Mr. Sodon has made no move at all. But I would not be surprised if he does not come down with a handsome offer, once he knows that we are open to it. In fact I would not be at all surprised, Miss Tycherley, if we could not obtain thirty pounds an acre for your land.' He regarded his young client hopefully, wondering if behind that calm brow there was not a brain that was able to calculate to no small purpose. 'I do not suppose an extra six thousand pounds will mean a great deal to either his lordship, or to Mr. Sodon,' he added.

Mrs. Tycherley added six thousand pounds on to twelve and was dumb from sheer ecstasy. Eighteen thousand pounds ... Who could have dreamed only an hour ago that such a prospect would open out before them? Dear Tunbridge Wells, with its charming shops in the Pantiles, and the orchestra that played there during the summer months, and the Ladies' Coffee Rooms—so different from the London coffee-houses where only gentlemen were allowed to enter—How delightful it would be to return there and be welcomed by all their friends!

Mr. Snuff got up. 'May I conclude that I have your permission to proceed with the business?' he asked Harriet, rolling up the plan of Beauregard and tying it again with its pink tape. 'Would you like me to write to his lordship's man of business, stating our terms for the sale of the property?'

'No, thank you,' said Harriet, suddenly making up her mind.

He stared as if he could not believe his ears. 'I beg your pardon?' he said.

'I said, no thank you,' said Harriet firmly, while Mrs. Tycherley's castles tumbled about her.

'Oh Harriet!' she cried in anguished tones. The charming house, the neat garden, the gossip in the mornings on the Pantiles outside the delightful little shops ... was it all to be a mirage, vanishing with the new drawing-room furniture and the breakfast parlour carpet?

Harriet turned to her and took her hands. 'Mamma,' she said pleadingly, 'I know this must sound absurd, but I have never owned any land in my life before, nor a house, and I would like to go and visit it just once before I dispose of it all to a stranger.'

Mr. Snuff and her Mamma breathed again.

'Well, I daresay there may be a housekeeper there still,' said Mrs. Tycherley and the lawyer agreed that there was a Mrs. Pells, who acted as housekeeper and cook at the Manor, and her husband, Pells, who was the butler.

'I do not think there are any other servants there,' he added, 'though there might be a gardener and a groom outside. It has not been possible to keep maids at the Manor for some time.'

'Too lonely, I expect,' said Mrs. Tycherley wisely. 'Young girls would not be happy in such a situation.'

Mr. Snuff did not say that it was Mr. Walter's habits that had frightened the young girls away, not the loneliness of the situation.

'Then I would be obliged if you will write to Mrs. Pells and tell her to have the house ready for us by the end of this week,' said Harriet briskly. She smiled encouragingly at her Mamma. 'We shall be able to travel post again, dearest! And we can pay Mrs. Slatterly's bill and leave these horrible lodgings for ever. Oh Mamma, I feel as if Paradise has opened!'

Mr. Snuff wished that he could feel the same, but he fancied that a week or two at Beauregard Manor would be all that the ladies would need to convince them that their wisest course was to sell Harriet's inheritance to the highest bidder as speedily as possible. He promised to write to Mrs. Pells however and to have a post-chaise hired for them by Saturday morning, and then he bowed himself out, and soon afterwards his carriage moved away down the street with every small ragamuffin in sight after it.

Harriet watched it go, while behind her Mrs. Tycherley said wistfully, 'Of course I know it is your property, my love, and your money, and you must do exactly as you please, but don't you think you might be a great deal more comfortable in Tunbridge Wells? ... We had such delightful friends there, and it was such a select neighbourhood. You would have a social life there that you may not be able to enjoy in this old country house. It sounds very lonely, my love.' She thought of the rotting floors and the leaking roof and suppressed a shudder.

'Beauregard,' said Harriet softly, her eyes shining. The name was romantic and beautiful. She could see the old Manor House, with its few devoted retainers, waiting her arrival. She could see the village, full of kindly people who had always known and loved the family. She knew so exactly what it would be like.

And how could she sell it to either of her wealthy neighbours feeling as she did about it? And what did it matter if it was just a small 'parcel of land' dividing two great estates?

'I don't care a snap of my fingers for either of them,' she cried gaily, without explaining who it was she meant by 'them'.

Mrs. Tycherley returned to her memories of Tunbridge Wells and her dreams of drawing-room furniture and a new breakfast-parlour carpet. It was her habit to shut her eyes gently to unpleasant prospects, and she was certain that Beauregard Manor was a dreadful old house, full of draughts, damp and rats.

But she would never allow Harriet to go there without her—indeed, if she had been left the Tower of London she would have accompanied her there with scarcely a qualm —and she trusted to her young stepdaughter's common sense to see it without any rose-coloured spectacles once they were there.

*   *   *

It was the middle of May and it was warm that Saturday. The London streets seemed to be full of the smells of drains and soot and garbage and smoking chimneys and unwashed humanity.

Mr. Snuff had ordered a post-chaise from one of the largest livery stables in London for the two ladies, and John Tycherley arrived just before it was due to start to see that their luggage was strapped and ready to be secured on the roof, and the ladies themselves safely inside.

Mrs. Slatterly, whose bullying tones had assumed an almost oily smoothness during the past few days, was there to see them off, dropping curtseys whenever Mr. Tycherley looked her way, and begging him to remember that her parlour front was now vacant, with the dear sweet ladies gone.

'You were lucky,' John Tycherley told his niece, 'that the races were not on this week, otherwise I don't suppose Mr. Snuff could have procured a chaise for you for love nor money.' He smiled at Harriet affectionately. 'As I only received your letter yesterday morning I have not had time to say how delighted I am at your good fortune, my dear. But to tell you the truth, I never thought that my visit to Walter Beauregard could have this outcome.'

'*Your* visit, Uncle John?' Harriet was surprised. 'I did not know that you had met Mr. Beauregard?'

He looked slightly embarrassed. 'When your father died last year I turned over in my mind all the relatives who could perhaps help you and your Mamma to remain in Tunbridge Wells—if not in the house you were then in, at least in a smaller one so that you would not be forced to give up all your friends and leave the town. Unfortunately the Tycherley side of your family is woefully short of money, my dear, so that we could not do as much for you as we would have wished. So I went to see Mr. Walter Beauregard, and I laid the situation before him, reminding him that as you are Sir Robert's grand-daughter the property he enjoyed should have been yours. I could see in a very short time though that no help was to come from that quarter. He laughed in my face and said that he had no money to throw away on widows and orphans and "Tycherley scum". And then he seemed to pull himself up and gave me a sharp look and asked if you were pretty.'

'Oh poor Uncle John! What did you say?'

'I said you were of course . . . and so you are to me, my dear!' He patted her hand affectionately.

'Dear Uncle John!' she said smiling. 'And then?'

'Why then he said "I tell you what I will do, I will make her my heir! In fact, I will make a will at once, in your presence, sir, and my servants shall witness it." He sat down at a writing table and wrote on a sheet of paper for a few minutes, only pausing to ask your full name and your father's, and when he had done he read it to me. It sounded a lot of gibberish, with grand legal phrases slipped in here and there, at which he laughed immoderately. The butler and housekeeper witnessed his signature, and he sent out for brandy in which to drink your health, but I did not join him. I could see that he had been drinking before I arrived, and I was angry with him for what I took to be a tipsy joke at your expense. Walter Beauregard was a young man, not yet thirty, and in all probability he would marry and have children. I thought he had chosen a cruel way to demonstrate to me that you had little to hope for from him, and I came away sick at heart and wishing that I could do more. I never expected that we should hear any more of the matter, and until I had your letter yesterday I had no idea that he was dead. Indeed, had I known of it sooner I very much doubt if I would have given it a second thought, concluding that the absurd will he made that day would have been destroyed as soon as it was made. But it was not destroyed, and he died unexpectedly, long before his time, and Beauregard is yours! I wish you joy of your inheritance, my dear.'

'Thank you, Uncle. When I wrote to you I wrote also to Mr. Snuff asking him to see that you were repaid for your generosity to us over this past year as speedily as possible. I know how hard it has been for you to meet our financial burdens when you have enough of your own, and I am determined that Mr. Snuff shall pay you back every penny out of the Beauregard estate, with my very grateful thanks.' There were tears in her eyes as she spoke, and though he brushed it aside she knew that he would be glad to have the money repaid. He had been so uncomplaining and cheerful throughout however that she could only guess at the strain it had meant on his resources. She added eagerly:

'But you have seen Beauregard, Uncle. What is it like ... the Manor and the village?'

He hesitated. 'There is scarcely time to tell you now, and you must not forget that my opinion was prejudiced by my dislike for its owner at that time. I saw it all in the worst light ... And here is your Mamma, and the horses are getting restive. It will be best if I leave you to form your own impression when you see it today. Being the owner of a property can transform it wonderfully, so I am told.'

And then Mrs. Tycherley was settled into the carriage, her smelling bottle was found and put into her hand, a shawl placed round her shoulders in case she should catch a cold from draughty windows, although the chaise had been in its time an excellent carriage, and the windows fitted well into the frames. The usual little band of ragamuffins had gathered, open-mouthed at so much splendour, while Harriet sprang up into the seat beside her Mamma, being delayed at the last moment by the young gentleman from the second floor back who thrust a wilting bunch of flowers into her hand and told her in mournful tones that Gale Street would not be the same without her. A further delay was caused by Mrs. Tycherley searching for her purse, which was found, after looking everywhere else where she fancied she had put it, in the pocket of her dress, so that she might empty it of its coppers and throw them to the children.

And then, with a wave from Mr. Tycherley, a sweeping bow from the young actor, and a succession of bobs from Mrs. Slatterly, they were off, with Beauregard at their journey's end.

3

There was not a great deal of traffic stirring at that hour, and once the odorous Thames was crossed Harriet let down the window on her side, eager to see everything that she could on the journey. A journey of any kind, she maintained, was an adventure.

Soon the London streets were left behind and they were driving through the charming little town of Clapham, with its delightful common and the large and beautiful houses that fronted on to it. Mrs. Tycherley remarked with a sigh that it reminded her of Tunbridge Wells. 'The common, you know, and those beautiful houses ... I should say much the same sort of people live here, people like the Miss Datchetts and dear Lady Piggott.' Harriet tried not to think that it would be a good thing if they never set eyes on the Miss Datchetts and Lady Piggott again.

'I had forgotten how lovely the country is in May,' she said. 'Look at the buttercups, Mamma ... and the oak is out before the ash. We are going to have a fine summer.'

The oaks made patches of gold against the bright green of beech, and the scent of the hawthorn flowers drifted in at Harriet's window, driving out the smells of leather and straw and mustiness that lingered in hired carriages.

Mrs. Tycherley was surprised to find that the village of Sutton now had large houses lining the road, each house with its big garden and handsome stabling.

'My first husband used to say they belonged to stock jobbers,' she told Harriet. 'He had a great contempt for such people, but I suppose the poor things have to live somewhere. And I daresay it is as easy for them to drive up to London from Sutton as it is from Richmond. I remember he took me once to Richmond when the cherry orchards round Kew were in bloom. It was a most charming excursion. Richmond was as select as Tunbridge Wells in those days, though I remember hearing that a great many rough people went out there on Sundays. I like the countryside of Surrey. It is a very neat and tidy countryside, and I like neatness and tidiness in nature. I do not care for a wild and rugged landscape ... I hope Beauregard will not be too wild and rugged, my love. I must confess I do not find such landscapes very comfortable.'

'But I am sure Beauregard is beautiful,' said Harriet. It had such a romantic name. 'When was the last time you travelled post, Mamma?'

'When I set out on my wedding trip with your Papa,' said Mrs. Tycherley promptly. 'And he had not the money to pay for it, so that he was forced to pawn his watch. How he laughed! He always made such a joke of everything, dear man ... Of course, travelling post *is* very expensive. I wonder how much Mr. Snuff paid for this? Did he tell you?'

'No, Mamma, and I did not ask. Let us not spoil the journey by thinking about money. Let us think instead how much nicer it will be to have our own carriage again. Mr. Snuff did not say anything about carriages and horses being in the Beauregard stables, but there are sure to be some there.'

'Oh yes, Mr. Walter Beauregard must have kept his carriages, my love. And even if there are none, when you sell the estate you will be able to buy as many as you want. Eighteen thousand pounds is a great deal of money, Harriet!'

'It is,' agreed Harriet cheerfully. 'A very great deal of money for such a small parcel of land ... You would not think that two gentlemen, with so many acres of their own, would trouble their heads about mine.'

Mrs. Tycherley glanced at her step-daughter uneasily. From the expression in her hazel eyes she fancied there might be more going on behind them than she knew, and she wondered what it was. There had been a similar look there in the old days at Tunbridge Wells, when Harriet had set her mind on doing something of which her father had not approved. She had been given to unexpected impulses, some of them ending disastrously, like the time when she had brought that dreadful old musician home with her from the Pantiles, where he had spun a long story about being starving. Everyone, except the trusting Harriet, could see that it was drink he was suffering from and not starvation. She hoped she was not experiencing another impulse over this property in Sussex.

They changed horses for the second time at Reigate, and the new post boys took them on recklessly into the thick of the Brighton traffic. The road was now uncomfortably crowded, and every few minutes they were overtaken by flying mails, or by private carriages driven at speed, or, what was almost worse, they were stuck behind the heavier stage coaches and wagons carrying goods and farm produce, and the more cumbersome, old-fashioned family coaches, whose coachmen refused to be forced into the ditch by any post boys in England.

An hour passed before they left the Brighton road and turned thankfully into a quiet, meandering lane. The chaise had good springs and they felt the jolting and bumping caused by cart ruts was better than the clouds of dust and constant overtaking and anxiety of the smooth, macadamed surface they had left behind.

'I cannot think why everybody wants to be in such a hurry,' complained Mrs. Tycherley. 'I do believe speed to be the curse of our age. People who do not go so fast get there just the same, and with less fret to the nerves!'

Presently the lane forked and they turned on to a bleak expanse of common and not a cottage nor a hut in sight. The landscape now became more hilly, and sunshine and shadow chased each other over the slopes of the downs ahead. They left the common and made for a break in the hills to the south east, and after traversing several empty miles with only one hamlet to break the monotony, they came out on to the coast road and in sight of the sea.

Harriet had never seen the sea before and she exclaimed at its beauty: the wind had freshened and clouds were now massing into the sky that had been so deep and untroubled a blue when they left London a few hours ago. The sea was green and flecked with white horses, but where the sun caught it between the clouds it was all life and sparkling movement and she could not take her eyes off it.

The road along the coast was all too short for Harriet and she was childishly sorry when they left it and cut back inland, making their way now through the Weald with its pleasant farmsteads and meadowland and fields of growing corn, green as the surrounding grass, and after another hour's travelling they went back to the hills, climbing steadily and cresting them suddenly to come down to the coast again.

Here however the sea was pale and distant and had lost its sparkle, the sky above it had become grey and overcast, and the wind blew so cold that Mrs. Tycherley begged Harriet to close her window. The sunshine had now been left quite behind, the hills that lined the valley ahead were dark and grey, the clouds that massed above them hiding the skyline in mist.

The post boys took the road along the right hand side of the valley, and presently they came upon the village of Beauregard, set back and hidden from the sea by a belt of trees.

Now at the back of Harriet's romantic mind there lurked the thought that when the news of her impending arrival reached Beauregard the villagers would be waiting to welcome her, the women to bob respectful curtsies as the carriage passed, the men to touch a forelock. She almost expected illuminations in the cottage windows and a banner with the words 'Welcome to the Heir' to be slung across the village street, as it was when Wilfred Penderville was brought home in triumph to his inheritance.

But to her disappointment the village was empty as they passed through, the only inn, the Lobster Pot, shuttered and silent. The church and the Rectory next door to it seemed to be equally devoid of life, and it was quite pleasant to see the glow of the fire in the blacksmith's shop on the green, as there did not seem to be another spark anywhere. As for illuminations in her honour, or welcoming banners, they were conspicuous by their absence.

They went on up the road, which now became more

wooded, and after about a mile the trees met overhead, creating a dark tunnel, though the leaves were not yet fully out. At the end of this tunnel a high flint wall ran along the right hand side of the road, broken at one point by a small stream that flowed sluggishly under a hump-backed bridge to join the river below, the banks of the stream above the bridge hidden by thickets of trees overhanging the water.

The journey nearly at an end, the post boys hurried their horses towards the entrance gates where an octagonal Gazebo stood inside the flint wall, with a copper cupola above eight slender stone columns. One column had broken away, and the cupola sagged above it, like the hat of a drunken man tilted to one side.

Harriet stared about her, scarcely able to credit that this was her inheritance. The crumbling gates were thrust back into banks of weeds that must have prevented them from closing for years, and beyond them a ruined lodge stood derelict, overgrown with ivy and brambles, its windows sightless eyes, its roof open to the sky.

The carriage turned into a grassgrown track that had once been a well-kept road through parkland up to the Manor House, and as she caught sight of the lake beyond the Gazebo, its water hidden by weeds and rushes, and the fountain in the middle of it, in the shape of a stone shell held aloft by three stone cherubs, and evidently too choked to play, Harriet thought despondently that she knew what Mr. Snuff meant when he told her it would not be possible for her and her Mamma to live at Beauregard.

And then she glanced from the fountain to the house, and the rose-red brick of the twisted chimneys that rose pleasantly against the surrounding trees and the scrubby steep hill-side beyond them, and the momentary depression of her spirits lifted as she caught sight of two people standing in the drive outside the front door.

They had seen the chaise and they were waiting for

its arrival, while a groom held their horses. Here then was the welcome she had anticipated, and Harriet's friendly soul went out to meet them, so that she scarcely waited for the carriage to stop and the steps to be lowered before she was out of it and hurrying across the drive to greet her visitors.

The lady waited for the gentleman to speak first, and he came forward hesitantly, holding out his hand.

'Miss Tycherley?' he said, as if not quite sure of his welcome. 'My name is Beauregard . . . Edward Beauregard. I believe we are distant cousins.'

She looked up at him startled. He was much older than she had pictured him to be, a man well on in the thirties. His hair was thick and dark, touched with grey, he had dark eyes in a fine-featured arrogant face, and he was tall and broad-shouldered. His air of assurance and his age made her a little shy of him, while he was equally disconcerted by the directness of her gaze and the wide innocence of the smile she gave him. It was a nice smile, he thought, a warm and welcoming smile, and it made him feel guilty, because he should have been there on an errand of welcome, and he was not.

He turned rather hurriedly to introduce his companion, Miss Julia Sodon.

'We had no idea that you were expected here until your butler Pells told us so today,' he said apologetically, while Miss Sodon's eyes rested on Harriet's shabby clothes and unfashionable bonnet with some amusement. 'Miss Sodon wished to see the Manor, and so we rode over . . . to see what sort of condition it is in, you know.'

'Indeed?' The smile faded from Harriet's face as she saw the laughter in the lady's beautiful eyes. Miss Sodon was young, very lovely to look at, and very elegant, but she wondered what business it was of hers. She heard her cousin asking if she would be staying long.

'Pells said he thought you were probably coming for

a week or two, in order to select the things you wanted from the house,' he added.

'I have not yet made up my mind.' Harriet smiled faintly at the beautiful Miss Sodon. 'I do not know how long I shall stay.'

'I hope you will not be very uncomfortable,' said Miss Sodon, with a light concern for her that did not ring true. 'It is really in the most dreadful condition, Miss Tycherley. Nobody could ever contemplate living there again. It would be quite impossible.'

Harriet said nothing. Miss Sodon, she concluded, had never lived in Gale Street. Edward Beauregard, who had been watching his young cousin as if she puzzled him, now apologised once more for having come at such an inconvenient hour and said that they would intrude on her no longer.

'You will be tired to death after your long journey,' he said. 'I am staying with my sister, Liz Staveley, in Woodrington, for a few weeks, and I will come over and call on you and Mrs. Tycherley tomorrow if I may.'

Harriet said they would be pleased to see him, acknowledged their farewells with a slight curtsey and watched a moment more while the groom brought the horses forward and Mr. Beauregard clasped his hands to give Miss Sodon a foothold for mounting. She went up into her saddle with an ease and grace that the small, plump Harriet envied. Then Edward Beauregard was up on his mount in a flash and with a final salute to the new owner of Beauregard they were off, the groom riding some little way behind, and the lady and gentleman turning their heads to laugh together in a way that surprised Harriet by the degree of intimacy that it suggested.

She wondered if Miss Sodon's desire to marry into the aristocracy was quite as firm as her father's, and she watched them until they were out of sight with a feeling of envy for Julia. She rode so effortlessly and so easily, her slender figure seeming one with her horse, and she wondered what she was saying to Edward that made him laugh so much, and if it could be herself or her dilapidated house that they found so amusing.

For the second time that day a shadow was cast over the joy of possession, and as she wondered what Edward's sister was like, she hoped that she had not the same air of amused condescension that she had detected in Miss Sodon, because if she had she did not think she would like her very much.

And then Mrs. Tycherley called to her and she ran back to the chaise, putting the thought of their tiresome visitors behind her in the pleasure of accompanying her Mamma into her inheritance.

* * *

'Well, Edward,' said Julia Sodon as they reached the lane beyond the ruins of the lodge, 'what do you think of your cousin? Is she as you expected?'

He admitted that she had surprised him a little. 'I had not imagined her to be so young,' he said.

'She is a funny, old-fashioned, dumpy little creature,' said Julia smiling. 'You do not suppose that she imagines she will be able to live at the Manor?'

'If she does, she will be quickly disillusioned,' said Edward grimly.

'I would not live there for a fortune, even if it were habitable,' said Miss Sodon thoughtfully. 'Those dark rooms, with that black old panelling, all leading out of each other ... and the steps up and down, ready to trip you up ... and the smell of mildew and damp and cobwebs everywhere.' She shivered. 'My father is determined to pull it down if it ever comes into his hands. I wish I could tell him that young woman's intentions as to her property, but she would say nothing, would she? Did you elicit any information from Pells?'

'No. He was as evasive as he always is. I have never liked or trusted him.'

'Were there any of Mr. Walter's servants whom you could like or trust? I would have said they were like master like man ...'

'There were one or two who had been there in Sir Robert's day ... I hope they are there still for my cousin's sake.' He glanced at his companion impatiently. 'But all this has nothing to do with us.' He turned his horse to accompany her as far as the Buldrayling crossroads where he had to leave her. 'When am I to see you again, Julia? I am in Woodrington for so short a time.'

'It depends does it not on how often you wish to see me?' said Julia, with a provocative glance at him from under her feathered hat.

'You know I want to see you every day ... Not a day passes that I don't think of you ... don't wish to be with you ...'

'Tomorrow then ... perhaps.' She considered for a moment. 'Yes, I think I could meet you at the cottage tomorrow morning at twelve ...'

'Must it be at the cottage?' He frowned, his proud spirit hating any form of deceit and subterfuge. 'I don't like meeting you there in your old nurse's cottage. I would rather everything was in the open between us, Julia.' He wondered that their secret meetings were not as repugnant to her as they were to him, humouring the old woman with money left under a cherished vase on the mantelshelf, and bribing the groom who accompanied her on these visits, so that he would not talk about the man she met there. It not only humbled his pride but it made his love for Julia appear to be furtive and cheap when he wanted to publish it proudly to the world. 'Can I not see you at Buldrayling?' he asked.

'Frequent visits from you at Buldrayling would not

please Papa very much, Edward. The name of Beauregard is not a favourite with him.'

'Does he class me with Walter, then?'

'No, of course not, and neither does Mamma, so you need not look so angry. But if you came to visit me as often up at the Hall it would make things look rather serious between us, and I do not want to be serious ... not with you. I much prefer you to laugh with me!' She held out her hand and allowed him to take it and raise it to his lips. 'I have enough gravity from Crowley,' she complained when her hand had been returned to her. 'He is such a *very* serious-minded young man. I am glad that his father's place in Northamptonshire claims his attention just now, so that I am free to enjoy your stay in Woodrington.' She glanced at his downcast face impatiently. 'Where is the harm of meeting in old Nurse's cottage? If I do not mind it, why should you?'

He supposed that he must be content with the crumbs that fell from Crowley's table, and he knew that her parents felt their beloved eldest daughter to be far too rich a prize for a country squire like himself. But when he was with her he could remember nothing except that she was his Julia, his lovely, wilful, charming love, and that if she would marry him he would love her till he died, no matter if old Sodon disinherited her. Indeed, to take her without a fortune would make him love her the more dearly, cherish her more tenderly, because of what she had given up for him.

There were times when he believed this might happen, in spite of the common sense within him that told him he was a fool, and he parted from her at the crossroads with the cheerful thought that he would be seeing her on the morrow.

4

The butler, Pells, was standing on the doorstep to welcome Harriet and her Mamma. He was a sleek-haired, short, thickset man, with sharp black eyes, and although he welcomed them with deference and said that his wife was just that moment coming, Harriet found that she did not like him very much. Maybe it was because she had never had a butler before.

'Miss Sodon and Mr. Beauregard coming like that, so unexpected, put us all back, Miss,' he grumbled. 'Otherwise everything would have been ready for you.' He shouted to the post boys to unstrap the luggage and bring it into the house, which they started to do sulkily, because it was not part of their business, which was only to drive the chaise. After a moment or two however a groom appeared from behind the house to help them, while Pells ushered Mrs. Tycherley and her step-daughter into a large square hall. The floor was of stone, the oak panelling on walls and ceiling black with age, and it was lighted only by a mullioned window with small, leaded panes and stained glass. A staircase led up from one shadowed corner steeply, and it was all very dark.

A door beyond the stairs opened and a woman came bustling forward to bob a curtsey and to introduce herself as the housekeeper, Mrs. Pells.

'I have a meal all ready for you, madam,' she told Mrs. Tycherley, as Pells left them with her. 'Knowing how tired and hungry you will be. I have a chicken roasted, and a gooseberry tart, and directly you are ready it shall be served in the breakfast parlour. It is warmer in there, and this old house strikes cold when the sun is down. It's the hills, you see, ma'am. They cast a shadow over it after four o'clock in an afternoon, however bright the day.'

They followed her into the breakfast parlour, a small and cosy room looking on to a tangled, windswept garden: this room too was panelled like the hall, and had a mullioned window and a stone floor, but the bright fire burning on the hearth was reflected in the dark old ceiling and made it a more cheerful apartment.

'That Miss Sodon thinks herself a Viscountess already,' complained Mrs. Pells, and Harriet liked her better for the scorn in her voice, although the woman's faded blue eyes were as shifty as her husband's. ' "Of course the house must come down," she says, looking about her with her nose in the air. "It's in a terrible state," she says. "Nobody could want to live here," she says.'

'That was where she was wrong,' said Harriet suddenly. She walked to the window to examine the garden and the tangled roses that grew into the rank brown grass of last year and the emerald tufts of this year besides. '*We* are going to live here, Mrs. Pells.'

'*You*, Miss?' Mrs. Pells stopped short, and her husband who was passing the door with Harriet's small portmanteau on his shoulder, let it slip to the floor with a bang. 'You are going to live *here* . . . at Beauregard?'

'Yes, Mrs. Pells. Mamma and I intend to make the Manor our home.' Harriet smiled brightly at the housekeeper, while Mrs. Tycherley could scarcely suppress a small wail of protest.

'Harriet, my love!' she cried softly. 'You cannot mean that?'

'Indeed I do.' If Harriet had never thought seriously before about making the Manor her home, her meeting with Miss Sodon would have decided her. She nodded encouragingly at the Pells, and then it dawned on her that the delight she had thought them to be feeling was as lacking as the villagers' welcome. She was able to read astonishment in their faces, coupled with consternation, but that was all. For some reason that she was not able to comprehend her desire to live in her house, instead of selling it to be razed to the ground, was not popular with her servants.

The next moment however Mrs. Pells had recovered herself. 'That will be very nice I'm sure, Miss,' she said in a smooth way that reminded Harriet of Mrs. Slatterly in her more ingratiating moments. 'To have the dear old house lived in again, and by such lovely ladies as yourselves ... We will be thankful for it, won't we, Pells?'

'Thankful is the word for it, Miss.' His obsequious manner returned swiftly and he picked up the portmanteau and bore it away. 'Show the ladies their rooms, Sarah,' he said as he went. 'They will like to see them I'm sure, before they dine.'

They followed Mrs. Pells back to the hall and up the steep oak staircase to the next floor. Here the floors were of oak too and as uneven as the stone ones below. A corridor stretched from one side of the house to the other, and off it one or two doorways were set deep and square in the dark panelling.

Mrs. Pells stopped in front of the first of these and opened the door into a large bedroom, with casements opening over the park, and another that led into a small dressing-room. This second room had only one other door, into another bedroom beyond, as large as the first. Harriet found all three rooms charming with their crooked casements, the faded chintz curtains at the windows and on the beds, and the old-fashioned furniture. Fires were burning on the hearths of the rooms and Mrs. Pells went through, making up each fire and shutting the windows.

As she did so Harriet suddenly saw what she had meant when she said that the sun left the house at four. It was striking four on the stable clock and although the clouds had dispersed and there was sunshine on the tops of the distant hills, here where the valley narrowed the shadows were already deep and impenetrable. In a nest of trees sunshine could filter through, but nothing could get through those chalky hills.

It gave her a sudden feeling of isolation and cold, and she left her Mamma to admire the appointments in her room while she went on through the dressing-room to the room that was to be hers. After a few minutes Mrs. Pells followed her and Harriet turned from the window to ask: 'How long is it since my cousin, Mr. Walter Beauregard, died?'

Mrs. Pells appeared to think a moment before she replied. 'It must be three months or more, Miss,' she said then. 'It was February when it happened.'

'He was ... drowned, I think?' went on Harriet.

'Yes, Miss. He was found in the lake one morning ... Very sad it was ... We were very upset.'

'In the lake?' Harriet felt her flesh creep a little as she looked at the distant lake with its cherubs and its fountain, now only a dim grey shape in the evening light. 'But ... is it very deep then?'

'In places it is, Miss ... Very deep!' Mrs. Pells poked the fire cheerfully. 'And now if you will excuse me, Miss, I will leave you to help your Mamma to unpack, while I see to the dinner. Everything will be ready when you wish for it.'

She bustled away and Harriet went through the intervening dressing-room to her Mamma's bedroom. 'What do you think of it, Mamma?' she asked.

Mrs. Tycherley was torn between the handsome appearance of the rooms and their quaint old furniture and pride in her step-daughter's inheritance—Lady Piggott's house had been nothing like this—and a feeling that a house in dear Tunbridge Wells would have been cosier to live in.

'It is a beautiful old house,' she said uncertainly. 'And I daresay I shall get very fond of it in time, love. Not that I care for the country very much, but then we appear to have near neighbours, do we not? ... That Miss Sodon ... and Mr. Edward Beauregard. I wonder that they did not stay for a little ... but he seemed to be anxious to be gone. What was Mrs. Pells saying to you just now? I heard something about the lake I thought ...'

'She said it was deep in parts.'

'Then pray do not venture near it, my love. You might fall in and I do not know how we would get you out, because there does not seem to be anybody about. I have seldom seen a more deserted spot than this, Harriet.'

Harriet said she was hungry. 'And I am sure you are too,' she added. 'Everything will look much nicer after a good meal.'

Their dinner was certainly a good one, improved by a French wine of excellent quality, which, upon inquiry, Pells told them the late Mr. Walter had bought from a friend in the Customs Office in London.

Harriet spent the evening in unpacking, while Mrs. Tycherley talked to Mrs. Pells about Tunbridge Wells.

That night Harriet slept soundly, but her Mamma, partly no doubt because of the regretful memories that her conversation with Mrs. Pells had brought back to her, was awake until the dawn.

Mrs. Tycherley was a townswoman, and to her the country was full of terrors: cows were frighteningly large, bulls were given to chasing people across fields and goring them to death, cockerels crowed their loudest in the dawn, putting an end to sleep, and geese came hissing at you across village greens before you knew what they were about. Country creatures in Mrs. Tycherley's eyes were full of unpleasant surprises, and most of them were agreed upon one thing, a desire to run after any unprotected female in their vicinity.

She lay awake behind her bed curtains quaking, as the owls hooted in the trees outside, and thinking she heard rats gnawing the wainscoting, and mourning dear Tunbridge Wells, and wondering if she would ever see it again. In the morning however the sun was up, and unhindered by the hills at that time of day, the dark old house was drenched with light. After breakfast Harriet decided to explore her new home and her Mamma went with her.

It was an L-shaped building, and Pells took them round, opening up the south wing for their benefit with the unnecessary information that the rooms there had not been used for years. The smell of mildew and the festooning cobwebs would have told them this without any word from him. On the ground floor however they were particularly charmed with the saloon, a handsome apartment that ran the length of the wing, and had been used in Sir Robert's day as a ball-room. It was marred now by a large portion of the ceiling that had fallen away in one corner, but it was still imposing with the carved alabaster chimney piece that reached to the cornice. In the alabaster, and again in the lozenges in the finely moulded ceiling, the Beauregard coat of arms was represented several times over, incorporating a fox and a hare, the two animals being carved on the chimney piece and forming the central motifs of the lozenges. The furniture in the room was in the French style, with gilded chairs and marquetry tables hidden away under their holland covers, and long mirrors and great glittering chandeliers draped in muslin with dust brown in the folds. The long windows with their deep window seats looked out to the neglected gardens, and were framed in honeysuckle and roses in bud.

Above the saloon, reached by a separate staircase, there was a picture gallery, and above that again, the great gallery of the house, now divided up into a series of lumber-rooms, mostly full of Walter's clothes and personal belongings.

They came back thankfully to the main part of the

house and the large gloomy dining-room with its portraits of past Beauregards staring down at the newcomers in aristocratic astonishment. From there it was but a step to the pretty, shabby drawing-room, the cheerful breakfast parlour, and the library with its shelves only half-filled with books.

'Mr. Walter was not fond of reading,' Pells said. 'I never saw him with a book in his hand. He sold most of Sir Robert's library.' He took them on to the kitchen quarters, which were large and had been intended for many scullery maids and several cooks, and they inspected the pantries, the larders, the cupboards full of china and glass and silver, and they glanced in at the housekeeper's room, which Harriet noticed was small and cosy with a cheerful fire burning, and a strong smell of tobacco.

Pells did not take them down to the cellars, but hurried them past the heavy iron door instead. 'The stream floods the cellars here in the spring, so that they are four foot deep in water,' he told them. 'There's rats down there too. They come in from the river banks.'

'Did you say rats?' faltered Mrs. Tycherley.

'Yes, madam. If you hear splashing down there and bumping about you will know what it is.' Pells smiled grimly and Mrs. Tycherley said she would like her smelling bottle.

While Harriet went to find it, Mrs. Pells, who was busy cooking with the help of an old crone from the village, came out of the kitchen to tell her husband how much Mrs. Tycherley had liked Tunbridge Wells. 'Such pretty country,' she said. 'This must seem very bare and bleak after Tunbridge Wells.'

'Ah yes.' Mrs. Tycherley sighed nostalgically. 'I would dearly like to go back there, Mrs. Pells. I had such delightful friends as I told you.'

'Perhaps you will go back there, Madam,' said Mrs. Pells consolingly, 'and sooner than you think.' She exchanged a glance with her husband and then as Harriet returned with the smelling bottle she went back to her cooking.

Mrs. Tycherley settled herself in the drawing-room with her needlework while Harriet went out to the stables alone. She found the groom that she had seen the day before in the yard, sweeping up the leaves that had drifted against the closed doors to the stables and coach houses, and lay there in such sodden heaps that she wondered how long it was since they had been swept up last. If Walter Beauregard had often been the worse for drink his servants could scarcely have been expected to do their work well.

The man told her his name was Rivers, and she asked him with some briskness to show her the carriages.

He put down his broom and glanced at her in a surly fashion: he was a man of forty-odd years, with a dark face in which sullenness seemed to predominate. But he went quickly enough to open the coach-house doors, and showed her the carriages there.

There were four of them, all except one, a gig, looking as if they had not been used for some time. She thought however that an old-fashioned chaise, if it were cleaned and polished and the caked mud washed from its wheels, might serve her and her Mamma for drives about the country lanes.

She told the man what was in her mind and he agreed that the chaise had been purchased in Sir Robert's time for the use of any ladies who were staying in the house. She told him to see to the cleaning of it and asked if there were any horses.

'No,' he said, adding 'Miss' after a moment as if it were dragged out of him. She glanced at him with more attention. The man was resentful of something, so much was plain, but there was an openness in his face that was lacking in Pells's and she thought he might just not like taking orders from a woman.

'What has happened to the horses?' she asked. 'How many did Mr. Walter have here?'

He told her there were four, two for riding and two for the carriage. 'Mr. Walter only used the gig, but he drove his horses hard and fast. The week before he died all the horses was seized by the horse-dealer he bought 'em off in Woodrington,' Rivers went on. 'They hadn't been paid for, you see, Miss, and folk can't wait for ever for their money . . . not even thieving rascals like horse dealers and such.'

'I shall have to buy a horse then,' Harriet said, knitting her brows. 'I daresay Pells will be able to tell me how I should set about it.'

'Pells?' He laughed scornfully. 'He don't know one end of a horse from t'other, doesn't Pells. He comes from London, and Mrs. Pells too.'

She was not surprised. The butler and his wife had the air and speech of townspeople, and she wondered what had induced them to bury themselves down here in a country house so far away from town life. It was not as if there could have been many guests at the Manor House during Walter's time to supply them with pickings.

'Did Mr. Walter have many friends visiting him?' she asked.

He smiled grimly. 'The friends he had were not the sort to bring horses and carriages with them, Miss,' he said. 'Nor did they bring servants with them, neither, if you understand me.' His eyes met hers significantly and the blood ran up into her face.

'I hope I do not understand you, Rivers,' she said and turned her back on him and walked away to the house with dignity.

He watched her go with a rueful smile. That look was her grandfather's all over again, and he guessed that she would meet difficulty and danger with the same spirit that

44

had made her mother run away from the Manor House.

But that was twenty years ago, when he himself had been but a stable lad here at Beauregard, long before the old man died and Walter Beauregard came to fasten on to the Manor and its lands like an evil fungus that was still spreading out its rotten tentacles though he was dead and gone.

5

As Harriet entered the house she saw Edward Beauregard riding up the drive, and she ran to take off her bonnet and shawl with a feeling of pleasant anticipation. This feeling was not diminished when Pells showed him into the drawing-room a few minutes later: as she took his outstretched hand and answered his enquiries after them both she knew that she could like and trust him. Here at any rate was somebody who would be able to help her to solve the smaller and more pressing difficulties that she might encounter at the Manor House.

Mrs. Tycherley greeted him with delight, being always ready to welcome visitors, and Pells was sent for refreshment.

Mr. Beauregard apologised once more for his intrusion of the day before. 'My sister hopes to visit you in the next day or so,' he went on. 'She trusts that she may see you both at Woodrington before you return to London.'

'But we are not going back to London,' said Harriet, and as he sat silent trying to master his astonishment she went on quickly, 'I intend to make the Manor my home.'

'She has fallen in love with it,' said her Mamma, smiling at her fondly. 'She says she will live here for the rest of her life.'

'Good God!' The ejaculation escaped Edward Beauregard before he could stop it and he apologised. 'The fact is that you took me aback, ma'am!' he explained.

Harriet said that she could not think why everyone was so surprised because she wanted to live in her own house, and there was an obstinate set to her chin that her cousin privately deplored, having seen it before, as Rivers had, in her grandfather. He agreed however that it did not seem very reasonable.

'But when my sister and I heard that our cousin Walter had left the property to a female cousin who resided in London, we did not think it likely that she would care to live in such an isolated spot on what was left of the Beauregard fortune—if I may tread on such delicate ground. I am afraid that our cousin Walter spent money very freely.'

'In that he was like Harriet's father then,' sighed Mrs. Tycherley. 'I was a widow when I married Captain Tycherley, Mr. Beauregard, and my first husband had left me quite a comfortable little fortune, but my dear Alfred had spent it all by the end of our four years of happy married life. He was too generous, my dear sir ... far too generous.'

Whatever Edward might think of the ethics of being generous with other people's money, he only said dryly that he did not consider generosity to be Walter's besetting sin.

'Poor Mr. Walter Beauregard!' said Mrs. Tycherley. 'Mrs. Pells told Harriet that he was drowned in the lake ... Was he out in a boat then? It looks scarcely large enough for boating, charming though it is to be out in a boat on a lake in the summer. My first husband was very fond of boating.'

'It was not summer, ma'am,' Mr. Beauregard reminded her. 'And he was not in a boat.'

'Then how was he drowned, sir?' asked Harriet.

He did not answer for a moment and then he said with some deliberation, 'I believe he was fishing.'

'Fishing?' Mrs. Tycherley was astonished. 'But what for?'

'Eels, I expect, ma'am. They are in their prime in February.'

Mrs. Tycherley shuddered and said she had only eaten eels once in her life, and they had made her extremely ill, whereupon Mr. Beauregard laughed unfeelingly and said that eels were very good to eat if you had a fancy for such things, but they had to be cooked just so, and he went back to studying his dumpy little cousin as if he were wondering if she really was the bread and butter miss that she appeared to be that morning.

And then Pells appeared with a decanter of wine and some thin biscuits made by Mrs. Pells, and as the butler poured out the wine and handed it round on a silver tray Mrs. Tycherley said she hoped it was as good as the wine they had the night before. 'If it is I can recommend it to you, Mr. Beauregard. It is French, I believe ... a charming wine. I understand that the late Mr. Walter Beauregard had a friend in the Customs Office in London, who was good enough to buy French wines for him ... At the Customs House Sales, you know.'

'Indeed?' Mr. Beauregard glanced at Pells's wooden face as he took his glass from the tray. 'I had not heard that before.'

Pells's face remained immovable, and Harriet was glad that her cousin had transferred his attention from herself to the wine. She had found his gaze disconcerting, and she wondered if he had been comparing her with the beautiful Miss Sodon, and wished that she could find something witty or original to say to him, but the storehouse of her mind, never as well stocked as she would like with treasures of wit, seemed emptier than usual that morning.

Her silence passed unnoticed however as Mrs. Tycherley chattered on happily about the wine.

'I remember my first husband had a friend in the Customs Office in London ... the Port of London, I believe ... and every now and then there would be sales of contraband goods held in the King's Warehouse there. They were sold off quite cheaply, because of course the Customs Service only wished to make what was due to them from the unpaid duty. This friend of my husband's used to visit us frequently in London, where we were living then, and he always brought us something—French silks and lace for me, and wines and brandy for my husband. Such a charming man ... And then he decided to emigrate to Australia, I don't know why. It was quite a sudden decision I believe. I remember my husband saying at the time that the Government was paying his passage for him, so they must have thought highly of him, mustn't they? That was just before we moved down to Tunbridge Wells.'

Mr. Beauregard said that he thought quite a few Customs officials were helped by the Government to find free passages to Australia, and then he turned to Harriet and asked if there was anything he could do for her. She hesitated before admitting that there was something, if it was not too much trouble.

'I want a little horse for the old chaise in the stables, so that I can drive Mamma out sometimes. It will have to be a mild little mare, I think, with gentle ways, because I am not accustomed to driving an animal with too much spirit. I do not know how much it will cost, but Mr. Snuff gave me quite a lot of money for my own personal needs before I left London, and I daresay I could pay for it out of that.'

'We had a dear little mare in Tunbridge Wells,' said Mrs. Tycherley. 'Jenny, her name was ... a sweet little creature. Harriet drove me everywhere when her Papa was not able to do so. There are no livery stables in Beau-regard, are there? In Tunbridge Wells there were such nice livery stables, and the grooms there were so obliging. I had no hesitation in disposing of Jenny to the proprietor because I knew she would be well-treated.'

Edward Beauregard said that the nearest livery stables were in Woodrington, but he would be happy to do what he could for his cousin. His brother-in-law had said some-thing the night before about a mare that was for sale, but she might be too large for the carriage in question. 'I will look at it before I go,' he said.

Harriet took him out to the stables, deserted now be-cause Rivers was having a chat with Edward's groom in front of the house, and he said he would see the mare him-self and judge of her size for the carriage. 'If she is right for the chaise you would be able to ride her as well,' he told Harriet. 'She is used to being handled by a lady.'

Harriet said regretfully that she could not ride.

'Then you must learn at once!' he said smiling. 'You cannot live at Beauregard and not ride!'

'I have no objection to riding,' she assured him, 'if you will be kind enough to tell me where I am to find a teacher?'

'You have one in front of you.' He thought it was the least he could do for the child. 'I shall be in Woodrington for a little while yet and I will be happy to be your teacher.' Was not Beauregard on the way to the cottage in the Weald? 'I don't promise that I shall be an easy one. I never allow an animal to be mismanaged: there must be perfect accord between horse and rider.' He saw that she was regarding him in a puzzled way. 'Does that not meet with your approval?'

'Oh yes. I was only wondering if you lived with your sister?'

'No. I have a house in Norfolk, left me by my grand-father, your grandfather's brother. It was too flat a county for my father, who could not be torn from his beloved Sussex downs—folk say that you have only to stand on a footstool in Norfolk to be able to see across the county. But there is a stringency in the air that I love.' He paused thinking of the bite in the wind coming from the icebergs of the North, and the way the poppies set the fields on fire in the summer, and the North Sea, a darker blue than anything to be found on the Channel coast, and cold on the hottest day. 'So I divide my days between Norfolk and my sister in Woodrington. Our parents died when we were children and we have always been closer to each other than many brothers and sisters.'

'I have never had a home of my own until now.' Harriet's young face was suddenly serious and her hazel eyes were dark with memories that he felt to be not entirely happy ones. 'Until I was fourteen I can remember nothing but lodgings, and then Papa met dearest Mamma and married her, and we went to live in her house in Tunbridge Wells. But although she welcomed me so kindly and I came to love her as much as I know she does me, I never felt that her house was my home. I always felt that I was a visitor there, perhaps because I had moved about so much in lodgings before.' Her eyes met his gravely. 'So will you please forgive me if I cling to the Manor? It has an air of a home ... though it *is* large for two ladies living here alone, and it is shabby and neglected and the rain comes through the roof. But it was here that my mother was born and brought up.'

The words, simply and sincerely spoken, won him over. Although he considered her decision to be unwise, he had not the heart to oppose it. It would be churlish indeed to refuse this small and sturdy plant the chance to send down its roots.

'My dear little cousin,' he said gently, 'I hope with all my heart that you find the happy home you anticipate here. I see no reason why you should not do so. The

Manor has known happiness in the past. And now,' he added, 'let us talk of your riding lessons.'

'Oh yes.' Her eyes sparkled. 'When shall we begin?'

'There is the small matter of buying a suitable horse first,' he reminded her. 'But directly that is done I will come over and see you again.' As they walked back to the house he asked her how many servants she had there.

'Five,' she said with a rueful little laugh. 'It is sadly inadequate, isn't it? And that includes old Cookson, the head gardener. He is a dear old man but he told me this morning that there were ten under-gardeners here in my grandfather's time. For the rest there are the Pells, and an old woman from the village, and Rivers in the stables. And that is all.' After a moment she added, 'I like Rivers, though he is brusque in his manner.'

'That is only his way. He means nothing by it.' He looked down at her with a queer intentness. 'And the Pells? Do you like them also?'

'I like Mrs. Pells, but I cannot trust him. There is a sly reserve about him, as if he knows many things about the Manor, and our cousin Walter, that he will not tell.'

'That might be so,' he said dryly. 'The Pells were Walter's servants in London long before he brought them to Beauregard, but I think in their case a long term of service with one master ...' He broke off and she had the feeling he had been about to add 'And such a master' before he continued rather quickly, 'could be recommendation enough. Walter was too heavily in debt to be a generous employer.'

He said he would have a word with Rivers before he left. 'I know he is bad-tempered, but there are reasons why he should be so, and he is a local man. I believe he will serve you well.'

He parted from her in the drive promising that he would come and see them again in a few days' time, and as he passed between the entrance gates a little while later he glanced at the Beauregard emblems that were carved on the posts there, yellow with lichen and overgrown with moss, and he smiled somewhat grimly to himself.

'The wiliness of the fox and the swiftness of the hare . . .' It had always struck him as being particularly apt for his cousin Walter, but he wondered if it was quite as apt for little Harriet. She was open as the day, and he felt that she would like to look all round a problem before she would reject or accept it, and he wondered how she would fare at Beauregard. And then as he turned into the road that led past Buldrayling and on up over the hills until it dropped down again on the other side into the Weald where old Nurse's cottage was, he forgot about his cousin completely in the thought that Julia was waiting for him there.

* * *

She was angry because she had been early and he was late. 'Do you usually keep a lady waiting, Mr. Beauregard?' she asked.

He explained about his visit to the Manor.

'Oh!' she said disdainfully. 'The little, dumpy cousin!'

'Yes. The dumpy cousin.' He came across the little room to her and took her hands and held them to his lips. 'Julia . . .'

'Crowley is coming back next week,' she said and took her hands away. 'Papa had a serious talk with me last night. He begged me to remember that I had four sisters!'

'I do not see what that has to do with Viscount Crowley. He does not wish to marry you all, I suppose?'

She caught his arm and gave it a little shake, her anger gone like a summer cloud in her laughter. 'Oh Edward, how I love you when you say things like that! ... No, I'm afraid the Viscount only wants to marry me.'

'But you do not want to marry him?'

'No, I suppose not.' She sighed. 'Papa is anxious that we should all marry titles.'

'Titles aren't everything, my darling.'

'I know, but I cannot seem to make Papa understand that as well as I do!' She was suddenly provocative. 'You would not like to marry Mary, I suppose, or Isabella, or Caroline, or even Amelia ... ? She will be the prettiest of us all given time. You could wait for her, Edward!'

'I have waited for you for five years,' he reminded her. 'I fell in love with you when you were sixteen ... at your coming out ball.'

'Poor Edward ... ! Have I been very unkind to you?'

How could he say that she had, when she looked at him like that?

6

Happily married to the younger son of a gentleman who owned a large estate in the West Country, Liz Staveley asked nothing more of life than the love of her husband, the management of his house and the company of her three children, whom she loved to distraction. As for Humphrey Staveley, all he wanted was Liz, enough stabling for his horses, and days devoted to sport and his few acres, which he pretended to farm. It was never more than a pretence with him and he allowed his friends and his brother-in-law to laugh at him as they would.

When Edward Beauregard told his sister about Harriet's decision to make the Manor her home she was as surprised and dismayed as he was, and she asked him what he thought of their new cousin, now that he had seen her again.

'I think she is far too nice a child to have such a joke played on her,' he replied at once.

'You think Walter's will was just a joke then?'

'I am sure of it, and I wish that he had not done it. It may turn out to be the cruellest thing he did in the whole of his corrupt life.'

'I wonder if you are right?' Liz was loath to think ill of anyone. 'Walter was a strange man. I think we saw more of him than you did, because you were so much in Norfolk even before you quarrelled with him. When he was drunk he was unspeakable, but when he was sober he could be very charming.'

'Did Humphrey like him?'

'Oh, Humphrey had only two recommendations for him; that he was a first class shot, and a fearless rider.' She laughed ruefully. 'You don't think he had a belated sense of righting a wrong when he made that will? He must have known that Harriet had more right to the property than he had.'

'If you can believe that of Walter I am afraid I cannot.' He frowned. 'I wish Harriet and her Mamma had more servants. The Pells have been feathering their nest for years at Walter's expense, and now that there are no more pickings they will only stay as long as it pays them to do so.'

'Isn't old Cookson there still?'

'Yes, and Rivers, and one old woman from the village.'

'Oh dear! But Rivers is reliable, and Cookson is a good old man and devoted to the family.'

'His only fault is that he is old.' Edward continued in a worried tone, 'You and I can guess what it is that threatens those two ladies most in that remote old house. There is not much that I can do, but I have had a word with Rivers, and I have arranged to take Harriet riding when I have found her a horse. She must know how to ride, living out there, and I said I would teach her while

I was here, which will mean that I shall be over at the Manor three or four times a week. I hope I shall not be in Humphrey's black books for it. But I do not like it all the same. I wish she had not decided to live there.'

'She is determined about it then?'

'My dear Liz, Harriet has our Great-Uncle Robert's chin!' He laughed wryly and she laughed with him, and then he told her what Harriet had said about her childhood. 'Her father seems to have been an out and out rascal.'

'Yes, Mrs. Furlong told me he had a name for being a waster when he was young.' The Furlongs were the Staveley's neighbours at Chowton Hall, Chowton being a village four miles or so on the Beauregard side of Woodrington. 'When she first married and came to Chowton she became very friendly with Rose and she said she was certain Captain Tycherley only persuaded her to elope with him because he thought Great-Uncle Robert would never disinherit her. She was his only child after all.'

'And instead Great-Uncle Robert kept his word!'

'Unfortunately for poor Rose. She died soon after Harriet was born, so Mrs. Furlong said, because I told her we knew practically nothing about our cousin. She said she did not know how Captain Tycherley and the child managed to exist, because he sold his commission and the proceeds of that would not keep them for long. But exist they did until he met the lady who is now Harriet's stepmother.'

'Ah well,' said Edward smiling, 'I suppose the graceless fellow must have had some redeeming quality, or two women—no, three with Harriet—would never have been so devoted to him.'

Liz glanced at her brother, wondering if his interest in Harriet's riding lessons were entirely on her account, or whether he intended to make them an excuse for visits to a certain small cottage in the Weald. 'You say that Harriet has her grandfather's chin,' she said. 'Is she pretty?'

'Oh no, not in the least!' He laughed, thinking of Julia Sodon's description of her. 'A little pudding of a girl ... with a very charming smile, however, and quite nice hazel eyes.'

Liz realised that she would have to wait until she met Harriet herself in order to judge the young woman's looks. To her brother Miss Sodon's dark beauty was still the perfection of female beauty. She hesitated, wondering if she ought to tell him that they had been seen at the old nurse's cottage together, and then deciding to hold her tongue. He was so sadly mistaken in Julia, but he would never believe her, never listen to a word against her. And Liz was convinced that Julia was only playing with him, that she meant to marry a title, and that love did not have any real place in her life.

* * *

Edward's 'word' with Rivers seemed to have effect, because the next time Harriet spoke to her groom he was polite, and when she asked him what wages he was receiving and offered to increase them directly she knew what she could afford to pay, he said that as long as they were paid he did not mind if they were increased or not.

Upon further enquiry she was horrified to learn that over five years' wages were owing to him, and she said she would write to Mr. Snuff that day and ask him to see that all her late cousin's debts were paid. 'Because I look on them as mine now,' she added.

Rivers smiled grimly. 'Debts, Miss?' he said. 'But there's some debts a man cannot pay ... even with his life.'

She did not understand him, and thought it was because she was not accustomed to the ways of rough country people as she went back to the house to write her letter.

'They speak their minds,' she told her Mamma as she

wrote, 'and I daresay Cousin Walter did leave a lot of debts behind him. Well, if it is possible without selling the Manor and the land they shall be paid . . . and in full, no matter how long it takes me to do it.'

A few days later Edward rode over to the Manor, with his groom leading a little mare, Molly, that was declared at once by Harriet and Mrs. Tycherley to be the most beautiful creature they had ever seen. He stayed to see her harnessed into the chaise, and to verify the promise that had been made him that she really was as docile and gentle as a lamb, and then he took his leave. But once it was understood that Mrs. Tycherley and her step-daughter could now return visits, Liz lost no time in calling at the Manor.

Harriet found her to be not nearly so awe-inspiring as the beautiful Miss Sodon: she was a pretty young woman of twenty-eight, not very smartly dressed, with her brother's dark eyes and a placid smile that spoke of a sweet temper. Moreover there was an air of such sound common sense about her, and such a warmth and kindness in her welcome to them both, that from the first moment she met her Harriet loved her.

Mrs. Tycherley entertained her with stories of her friends in Tunbridge Wells, and was delighted when Liz said she thought Mrs. Furlong of Chowton Hall had been a Miss Datchett.

Liz Staveley's visit was the forerunner of others. The Rector of Beauregard, Dr. Midhurst, and his sister who kept house for him, came in the Rector's gig, and as they preserved a rigid silence where Walter Beauregard was concerned, Harriet wondered if he might have been as unpopular with his neighbours as he was with his servants, and for much the same reason. She determined to ask Mr. Snuff in her next letter if there were any tithes owing to the Rector of Beauregard.

In the meantime her lawyer expressed great concern at

her decision to stay at the Manor. He did not know what his lordship's man of business would say, but he was afraid that he would not like it at all. But if she had made up her mind to live there, then he would ask a young man by the name of Frank Elkington, a nephew of one of her farmers, to become her factor on a temporary basis. He pointed out that her grandfather had been a rich man and able to employ an agent for his estate, but the six hundred impoverished acres that Walter had left his cousin were no longer able to afford such a luxury. Young Frank Elkington had a good business head however, and he would collect the rents for her and settle her servants' wages out of such moneys as he received, and suggest such repairs on her property as were absolutely necessary.

'You would not think the place was mine,' cried Harriet as she set out for a morning ride with Edward on the morning that the lawyer's letter arrived. The little mare had shown herself to be as steady and governable as a mount as she was in the shafts of the chaise, and the riding lessons had started in earnest. 'Why cannot I collect my own rents and pay my servants myself, pray?'

'As for collecting your rents ...' He glanced at her humorously. 'Can you fire a pistol?'

'Fire a pistol?' She stared. 'What has that to do with it?'

'Because you must carry one and know how to use it if you intend to do your own rent collecting,' he said quietly. 'Beauregard's pretty lanes can harbour rough characters sometimes, especially in the winter months.'

She was chagrined, but she admitted the sense of what he said.

'As for young Elkington,' he went on cheerfully, 'I know the lad well. He is a nice young man and well accustomed to country ways. He collects the rents for a number of small land-owners on the far side of Woodrington.'

'How did my cousin collect his rents?'

'When he was sober he collected them himself, other-wise Pells did it for him.'

'Was that why the Pells have stayed so long, do you think?'

'It could have been one of the reasons, certainly.' He shot an amused glance at her: there was a shrewdness in this eighteen-year-old cousin of his that surprised him.

'You said just now that Mr. Elkington collects rents for land-owners near Woodrington,' she went on. 'But I thought the Merrington estate took in all that part?'

'Much of the land to the north of the town, and the town itself, is owned by the Marquis, but to the south and west there are several small land-owning farmers, each with a few hundred acres of their own, and these are the people that young Elkington serves. The Marquis employs his own agent—or agents, rather, because he has one for each of his estates I believe.'

'Mr. Snuff told me he had five in all. Where are they situated?'

'One in Northamptonshire, one in Derbyshire, one in Devon, one in Sussex here, and one in Lincolnshire.'

'You would have thought that was enough for him with-out my poor little parcel of land as well?'

'There is more in it than mere acquisitiveness. Our cousin Walter did not preserve his game because, having spent all your grandfather's money, he could not afford a gamekeeper. As a result, poachers came up into the Beau-regard woods, snaring and trapping game, and slipping through the broken fences to the Merrington estate on the one hand and Buldrayling on the other. The gamekeepers there could be as vigilant as they pleased, but as long as Walter was content to harbour the ruffians they could not catch them red-handed. I think that is the real reason why both your neighbours would like to see Beauregard in-cluded in their estates, because I dare say when the autumn is here poaching will start again and I do not see how you are going to stop it.'

'But I shall stop it all the same,' said Harriet, setting her chin, and again she won a glance of approval from her cousin. Though she had never mounted a horse until a week ago she was promising to be an excellent little rider, and he supposed it was because in this, as in other things, she was quite fearless.

As to the poachers, he thought, they would jump that fence when they came to it: she had a great deal yet to learn about Beauregard, and the farm labourers employed on it who starve throughout the winter when their work on the farms was no longer needed. Such men would not only turn to poaching to feed their wives and families. He could not tell Harriet this however without laying himself open to a charge of trying to scare her away, and the summer was in front of them, with the men employed in honest work, and the winter more than a quarter day away.

In the meantime he had to admit that there had been a great difference in the old house since she had been there. The windows were now opened to the fresh summer breezes, the cobwebs had gone, the floors and furniture were scoured and polished by two little maids from the village that had been hired to replace the old woman. The girls, rosy-cheeked and smiling, with new ribbons in their caps and their print dresses fresh and neat, ran to do everyone's bidding with the best will in the world, while the flowers with which Harriet filled the rooms helped to give the impression that the Manor had come to life again under the touch of someone who was prepared to love it.

'I would like to see the lawns mown,' she said regretfully as they turned back. 'But one old man like Cookson, however beautifully he may be able to wield a scythe, cannot make much headway there.'

'Sheep,' said Edward Beauregard.

'I beg your pardon?'

'Beg some of your farmers' sheep,' he said smiling. 'They will crop it closer than any scythe. I will take you to call on Mr. Price the next time we ride out together.' He pointed with his crop to some farm buildings on the far side of the valley. 'That's his farm, halfway up that hill. You will like him. He is a farmer of the old school, though I hear from Miss Midhurst that his daughters are much too up to date. She says the Rector thinks it will be the downfall of England.'

'In what way?' Harriet could not imagine how a farmer's daughters could ruin England.

'Why, the good doctor grumbles because he says every farmhouse has its parlour these days, where the farmer's daughters can sit over their needlework and learn to play the pianoforte. He says that in his young days the girls milked the cows and made the butter and skimmed the milk and looked after the poultry and helped their mothers to bake and brew, going to market with their fathers every week to sell their produce.'

'And are they not doing this now?'

'The Rector says not. He says they are all being made into fine ladies, taught nothing but how to spend their days in idleness, and that trashy novels lay about now on the parlour tables where there used only to be the family Bible.' He laughed. 'Liz tries to reassure him by telling him it is what we must call progress, but he remains convinced that no good will come of this sort of thing.'

'I am afraid I am not above reading novels myself,' Harriet said guiltily, her thoughts going back to *The Secret of the Pendervilles*. 'There was little else to do in London and Tunbridge Wells ... But here where everything is so beautiful I do not want to waste a moment ... I feel I must take advantage of every second that is mine.' She turned a shining face to him. 'I am so *very* lucky!' she said. 'I would not change places with any other girl on earth ... Not even with Miss Sodon!'

He shot a quick glance at her. 'Now why do you say that?' he asked quietly.

'Because,' she said with great frankness, 'it must be very wonderful to be Miss Sodon ... to have everything from birth as she has had it. Beauty, riches, charm ... Nothing has been omitted, has it?'

'Nothing,' he said.

'And she has a beautiful home ... Buldrayling *is* very beautiful, isn't it?'

'It is considered to be one of the finest places in England.'

'Ah ...! And there is a number of servants, I daresay?'

'There must be a very great many there.'

She sighed, and her six hundred acres, her crazy old house and the woefully few servants at Beauregard dwindled sadly until the thought of Gale Street sent her spirits soaring again. 'But I still wouldn't change with Miss Sodon!' she said.

'Who has been talking to you about her?' he asked. 'Liz?'

'Yes.' She glanced at him uneasily. 'When we visited her last week ... You were not there, you were out with Mr. Staveley that day, and Liz said how beautiful Miss Sodon was ...'

'Did she say anything else?'

'Only ...' Harriet's voice dropped, 'only that she wished you wouldn't ...'

'Wished I wouldn't what? Come, you've told me so much you may as well tell me all ...'

'She said she wished you wouldn't love her as much as you do,' said Harriet gently, and he saw her grieved face and smiled and put his hand over hers for a second.

'You *are* a nice child, Harriet,' he said. 'But do not, I beg, worry your little head over my troubles. You will have plenty of your own at Beauregard!'

They came into the Manor drive and he left her there

at the stables, with Rivers to help her down, and went his way, taking the long way back to Woodrington through the Weald.

7

A few mornings later as Harriet sat at work with Mrs. Tycherley in the drawing-room Mrs. Furlong came to call, sent by Liz and prepared on Rose Beauregard's account to welcome her daughter.

Harriet and her Mamma were delighted to see her: there had been a storm in the night and it was still raining, and the air outside was oppressive and still. Her visit made a welcome diversion.

She was a fat, jolly woman, and it soon transpired that as Liz said she was a sister of the Miss Datchetts of Tunbridge Wells.

'My sister Annie went there for the cure years ago,' she said with her jolly laugh. 'And it did her so much good that she and Emily decided to stay. My husband says it is the walk to the well every morning that cures Annie of her ailments, not the water she drinks!' She was able to tell Mrs. Tycherley that all her friends in Tunbridge Wells had been well through the winter, with the exception of Lady Piggott who had had several severe colds. 'But that is because she drives everywhere in her carriage,' she added. 'She will not walk a yard if she can avoid it, especially in the cold weather. I don't wonder that she catches cold.'

'She always caught such bad colds,' sighed Mrs. Tycherley. 'She suffered from her chest so much ... Poor dear Lady Piggott.'

After more enquiries after mutual friends Mrs. Furlong

turned to Harriet and began to speak of her mother.

'So pretty she was,' she said with a puzzled expression as if it was strange that her daughter could be so plain. 'Self-willed too and determined to have her way. She loved this old house and it must have broken her heart to leave it the way she did. But when Rose had set her heart on a thing nobody could gainsay her . . . not even her father. It was like steel meeting steel.'

'You knew her very well, so Liz said,' said Harriet, her eyes shining.

'I did, my dear. I was young too in those days and Rose used to come and confide in me, because I was more her own age. I was so new to my position then : my husband's family have been squires of Chowton for generations. It is a very comfortable little estate . . . about a thousand acres or so. Not very large, but overpowering to a girl brought up as I had been in the restricting circles of Cheltenham and Tunbridge Wells.' She smiled brightly at Harriet. 'I do not believe Beauregard is more than six hundred acres, although this house is considerably larger than Chowton. I do not care for very large houses. They are often damp—especially if they are situated near a river. My father-in-law pulled down the old house at Chowton, which was very dark and had a great deal of panelling like this in it. He built a fine new house on the site, with the long windows that are so much more fashionable. I do not care for these old mullioned windows.'

'The stream does run rather close to the house,' agreed Harriet reluctantly. 'And there *is* plaster coming away from the ball-room ceiling, but I think that is because it has not been used for such a long time.'

'The last time there was a ball at Beauregard it was for Rose's eighteenth birthday.' Mrs. Furlong smiled sadly. 'It was soon after that when she ran away and half the house was shut up. And then in Mr. Walter's day . . .' She broke off. 'Ah well, least said soonest mended where *that* gentleman is concerned, and I daresay you cannot believe everything you hear about him even so.' She glanced sympathetically at Mrs. Tycherley, and Harriet said with a spot of pink in her cheeks that she would be obliged if Mrs. Furlong would tell her what she had heard about her cousin.

'My dear, I have no right to say anything about him.' Mrs. Furlong spoke with a kindness that made her ashamed of her small outburst of temper. 'We were not well acquainted, and he did not encourage his neighbours to visit him. But he did not enjoy his own company either, and in order to divert himself it is said that he invited to the Manor certain of his London companions who could not be regarded as acceptable in any sense of the word. It has also been said that there was scarcely a young woman in the village that he did not attempt to seduce. I daresay that is why we have been surprised that a young relation of his could think of setting foot in the place after what happened here in Mr. Walter's time.'

Here was the truth at last, the same that had been hinted at in the stables by the groom Rivers. Harriet's flush deepened and she got up and walked to the window, standing there for a few minutes staring out at the rain-soaked drive.

The carriage standing outside the front door was a large one, and the horses in its shafts were expensive animals. It had a coachman and a groom and there was a footman in livery up behind. What could a lady who drove out in such a fashion know of the joys of owning a humble old-fashioned chaise and a little mare like Molly? She had always known security, and had not been dragged from lodging to lodging in the wake of a charming but irresponsible father. She turned to face Mrs. Furlong with a dignity that matched her own.

'As my cousin did not recognise my existence during his lifetime except to make a will in my favour, which my uncle is convinced he only intended as a joke in rather bad taste, I cannot see that my living here with my dear Mamma can make me any sort of a party to his behaviour. How he lived while he was here may be a matter of deep regret to me but it is scarcely my fault. I only wish to live at peace in the house where my mother was born and lived as a girl. Surely it is not wrong to wish to do that?'

Remembering Rose Beauregard, Mrs. Furlong could not quite suppress a smile. In just such a way would she have defended herself, indignation quivering under young dignity. She said soothingly that nobody had ever dreamed of connecting Harriet with her cousin's lamentable behaviour, and that everyone was only too anxious to welcome her to the neighbourhood.

'When the autumn starts your Mamma must bring you to the monthly balls at our Assembly Rooms in Woodrington,' she said as she took her hand in parting. 'And in the meantime I hope we shall see you at Chowton. Our eldest daughter Maria is eighteen in July and we shall be giving a ball for her then. I shall send you an invitation and I shall not take a refusal.' She was a most kindly woman, and would very likely have welcomed her just as warmly had she had the looks of her mother to outshine her own pretty Maria. 'Everybody will be dying to meet you, my dear, because whatever may be thought about your taste in coming to Beauregard, nobody can say a word against your courage. You are indeed your mother's daughter in that respect!'

And with this rather back-handed compliment she patted Harriet's cheek affectionately and went out to her carriage and was driven away.

It had stopped raining and Harriet asked her Mamma to accompany her in a walk in the park, but she refused, saying that she was tired after her sleepless night, and Harriet went off on her own. An overgrown path surrounded the park inside the railings that separated it from the approach to the house, but there was enough gravel remaining there for it to dry quickly. She had been walking for a few minutes when she saw Edward Beauregard riding up the approach: he stopped and asked if she were not coming for a riding lesson that day.

She shook her head, but she did not reply.

'The hills may be too wet and slippery,' he agreed and added persuasively, 'but we could keep to the lanes. The country is fresh after the rain.' And then, seeing her face, he dismounted, gave the reins to his groom, and vaulted the fence to join her on the path. 'Is anything wrong?' he asked.

'Why did you not tell me?' she asked vehemently. 'Why did you leave me in ignorance ... of my cousin's behaviour?'

His eyes met hers intently. 'What have you been hearing about him?' he asked, not without anxiety.

She told him of Mrs. Furlong's visit and her account of Walter, blurting it out like a schoolgirl confessing to a crime, her eyes bright with tears, her cheeks still flushed with indignation and shame.

'But all this has nothing to do with you,' he said comfortingly as she finished, and she had an odd notion that he had waited for her to tell him something more and was relieved because she had not. 'The man lived no worse I suppose than many others but he should have kept his way of living for London. Here in the country society is limited and gossip exaggerated, but he need not have taken his ladies to church, and neither need he have decorated his carriage whip with their garters. There are some things that it is not seemly for a man to do: one does not flaunt one's mistresses under the noses of the local gentry.'

'Was that why you quarrelled with him?' she asked, her anger fading a little, but the shame remaining.

He shrugged. 'I had no right to make his business mine. He was justified in turning on me. But I did not come

67

here to talk about our cousin Walter. Let us turn our attention to something a great deal more pleasant. Will you not come out for a ride?'

'I cannot,' she said sadly. 'Poor little Molly is lame.'

'Lame?' He was surprised. 'What has caused that?'

'I don't know. She was all right yesterday when we drove to the Rectory to take tea with the Rector's sister: while we were there Rivers said the landlord of the Lobster Pot Inn came across the green to say what a fine little mare she was ... But today she is not only lame but she does not seem well. I can see that Rivers is very concerned about her, though he will not say much.'

'My horses are too big and powerful for you to manage yet awhile,' he said, glancing back at his groom. 'Or else we could have our ride in spite of poor Molly.'

She thanked him and said she did not feel in the mood for riding. 'Have you not noticed how clear the hills are? We shall have more rain before long.'

'I will leave you to walk while you can, and I will go and see Molly,' he told her and hurried away to the stables where he found Rivers in the saddle room polishing harness.

'What is this I hear about Molly?' asked Edward Beauregard. 'Is she really sick?'

'No sir,' said Rivers grimly. 'Just exhausted.' He raised his head and straightened his back and stared at Edward angrily. 'I found her like it in the stable this morning ... She's been worked like as if she was a cart-horse, sir. Come and have a look at the sores on her sides where the tubs have rubbed her. I'd dearly like to catch the devils that did it to her.'

Edward Beauregard followed him into the stable and examined the little mare carefully and agreed with him. 'Any idea who it was?' he asked, his mouth rather taut.

'No sir. But I'm ready to swear that Dawlish does, coming across to me yesterday as he did while the ladies were

68

in the Rectory. Fawning over Molly here and saying what a nice little creature she was, and strong too by the looks of her. He'll feel the strength of my fist if he tries it on again I promise you.'

'I'll speak to him on my way home.' Edward looked about him. 'How did they get in?'

'They took the padlock off, sir.'

'I see.' He examined the lock from which the screws had been removed. 'It was hanging like this when you came this morning I suppose?'

'Yes, sir. It was a dark night, you see, sir, and there was that storm.'

'There's only one way to stop them and that is for you to sleep here in the old grooms' dormitory over the stables on the nights when there is no moon. Do you think your wife would be nervous to be left on her own?'

'She can go to her sister's in the village, sir.'

'And Pells? Will he be prepared to sleep here too? There ought to be two of you at least ...'

'Pells?' Rivers laughed scornfully. 'First sign of trouble and he locks his bedroom door and pulls the blankets over his head. He's craven right though, is Pells.'

'I was afraid he might be.' Edward considered for a moment or two and then he said, 'Do you know a man— preferably young and strong—who would help Cookson in the gardens during the day and sleep here at night?'

At first Rivers said he did not know anybody, as all the young men were out in the fields, and then he remembered a nephew who might take the situation. 'He's been working for the livery stables in Woodrington, but they don't seem to make much of a go of it these days and they've turned him off. I don't think he's much of a hand with horses, mind, but he's got plenty of spirit, has our Harry, and he'd think nothing of tackling a whole gang of ...' He broke off. 'I'll see him tonight and ask him anyway, sir.'

'And if he will come, engage him at once. His wages can be my business. I will write to Mr. Snuff and tell him what I have arranged and why. And if the lad should not be able to come find me someone else.' He was walking away when he stopped. 'Oh, and Rivers . . .'

'Yes, sir?'

'Get a new lock.'

'I will do that, sir.'

He went back to the house and stayed a few minutes to hear Mrs. Tycherley's account of the bad night she had had, what with the storm and doors banging in the wind.

'I got up once thinking I heard the stable gate bang,' she told him. 'But it was only the storm and the thunder . . . I think in the country one hears sounds more clearly than one does in a town—especially a quiet little town like Tunbridge Wells. Don't say a word to dear Harriet though, Mr. Beauregard. She is so happy here and I would not like her to think me nervous.'

He reassured her and took his leave, saying that he would return in a few days' time when Molly's lameness would have gone and Harriet could ride out again.

'Molly is not ill then?' said Mrs. Tycherley, her face brightening.

'No,' he said. 'She is not ill.' And he went his way, far from easy in his mind at leaving her and Harriet to the protection of the cowardly Pells. Rivers he knew he could trust, and by hook or by crook he would find somebody to move into the stables with him.

There was to be no meeting in the cottage in the Weald that day. Julia had sent a note early saying that her parents were leaving Buldrayling for their London house the following day, making the excuse of the Drawing-Room for Mary. *I am sure gossip has reached them about Nurse's cottage though, and they are afraid that our tame Viscount should hear of our meetings there,* she wrote. *'So they are removing me to London to be on the safe side. I will write to you, my dearest Edward. Your own Julia.'*

Feeling happier than he had done for some time, because it seemed as if he would be able to meet Julia openly in the London houses of his friends instead of belittling them both by the furtive meetings at the cottage, Edward rode down into Beauregard village to the Lobster Pot Inn and found the landlord there alone, polishing the tankards in the snug.

'I have just come from the Manor,' he said, brushing aside the man's offer to fetch him something to drink. 'That little mare of Miss Tycherley's has gone lame.'

'Indeed, sir?' Dawlish was blandness itself. 'Nice little creature, that, sir.'

'She is too nice a creature to be treated roughly and brutally.'

'Brutally, sir?' Dawlish breathed on a tankard and rubbed off a stain on his cuff. 'I don't think I understand you, sir.'

'I think you do.' Edward's voice was stern. 'She has sores on her sides as if she has been saddled with a heavy load, and she is exhausted and nervous ... Somebody has used her badly since yesterday, and it was nobody at the Manor. I have come to tell you, Dawlish, that I will not have this sort of thing. I do not care what Mr. Walter Beauregard countenanced up there, but those two ladies are not to be exposed to anything of the same sort. Do I make myself clear?'

Dawlish remarked that everyone knew the ladies at the Manor to be innocent as lambs. 'Have they complained at all, sir?' he asked.

'You know that they suspect nothing. They are, as you say, as innocent as lambs, and I will not have them led as lambs to the slaughter by you and your friends. You can pass the word round if you like and say it is an order from me.'

'I won't bring your name into it, sir, if you don't mind.' Dawlish turned his back on his visitor to replace the tankards on their hooks. 'There's some as wouldn't stop at much in Beauregard.'

'Is that a threat?'

'A threat? But why should I threaten you, sir? It has nothing to do with me.' His eyes met Edward's and fell away. 'There's some things that goes on in Beauregard that it is best to know nothing about all the same. It's best to keep quiet about 'em, if you know what's good for your health, sir.'

Edward did not answer at once, and then his voice though quiet was steely with anger. 'You and I may or may not know what is going on in the village, Dawlish,' he said. 'But Miss Harriet's mare will not be used again, and I am giving you this warning that the Manor is not to be used for anything in future, under any circumstances.'

The landlord remained sullenly silent, and Edward went back to his horse in a cold rage that kept him from seeing the Rector's salutation from his garden gate. Miss Midhurst said acidly that Mr. Beauregard, like his cousin Walter, appeared to like his friends at the Lobster Pot better than those at the Rectory, but the Rector only went on tying in the honeysuckle that had strayed over the gate and said nothing. He had heard, in the way he did hear such things, that Harriet's nice little mare was lame, and the look on Edward's face made him think that perhaps his visit to the Lobster Pot might have something to do with that circumstance.

After Mr. Beauregard had gone Mrs. Dawlish came out from behind the snug and said reproachfully, 'Did you use that mare last night, Dawlish?'

'If you listen behind doors, my girl, you'll hear more'n is good for you,' he said sharply.

'Yes, but did you?' she persisted.

'It was that Charlie,' he grumbled. 'He's more used to

handling carthorses. I told 'un not to load 'un too high, but we was in a 'urry. Come the first dark night the Coast-guards is all over the valley like flies.'

'But with the ladies now at the Manor it don't seem right,' said Mrs. Dawlish timidly.

'Makes it doubly safe, don't it? Nobody won't think of searching the Manor ... and it's as well they don't, be-cause there's a load of stuff there it will take weeks to get away. If chaps is hard pressed they make for the first safe place they knows of.'

'I don't like to hear you threatening Mr. Beauregard all the same. It might make him think about Mr. Walter more'n he do.'

'None of us laid a finger on Mr. Walter,' said the land-lord of the Lobster Pot positively. 'I'll take my oath on that. He was far too useful alive for any of us to wish him dead.'

'Somebody killed him.'

'Ah, and I can hazard a guess who it was too, the way the crazy chap opened his mouth in here before it hap-pened, swearing he'd kill every Beauregard in the country. You'd think that Nancy of his never went willingly to Mr. Walter, as we all know she did.'

'Aye, she was not a wench to risk hanging for,' agreed his wife.

'What I didn't tell Mr. Beauregard though,' said her husband in a low voice, 'was that Jake is back in the neighbourhood again.'

'Jake Linnet?'

'Aye ... Jake Linnet himself. And it's my belief he's far more of a threat to Miss Harriet's safety than a few casks in her cellars. If Jake should get hold of her one dark night she'll end the same way as Mr. Walter.'

8

Molly recovered and when Mr. Beauregard visited the
Manor at the end of the week Harriet told him that young
Harry Rivers was anxious to come as under-gardener to
old Cookson, and that she had written to Mr. Snuff to ask
if she could afford to pay the extra wages. Edward said
that he did not suppose they would present a problem,
and was glad to see the stalwart young man on the premises.

There followed a delightful spell of Arcadian weather,
when Harriet went riding or took her Mamma out in the
chaise. The chaise was much in demand at that time, because numbers of Mrs. Furlong's friends came to see for
themselves Liz Staveley's intrepid young cousin who was
prepared to settle down happily in the dilapidated old
Manor.

Edward kept his promise to introduce her to the farmers
on the estate, explaining with young Elkington's help the
contracts that had been entered into when they or their
fathers or grandfathers took the farms, and what the landlord's obligations were as well. He found her a surprisingly apt pupil, with a quick grasp of problems that
continued to earn his respect.

One morning after they had been out riding together
Rivers told him that Jake Linnet was back in the village.

'Of course we know Miss Harriet hasn't the same name
as Mr. Walter and yourself,' the groom said, plainly uneasy, 'but her mother was a Beauregard, and Jake don't
reason things out. He always was a bit soft in the head,
and from all accounts he's ten times more so now.'

'Do you think he is a real danger though?' Edward
smiled contemptuously. 'It was never proved that he had

anything to do with Mr. Walter's death.' He saw the doubt on the groom's face and went on with some impatience, 'Come, man, you know as well as I do that Mr. Walter drank far more than he could carry. He could have staggered into the lake that night and drowned without a soul being near him.'

'Why yes, sir, so he could … But Miss Harriet is different from Mr. Walter, isn't she, sir? She's a thorough nice young lady is Miss Harriet, and I wouldn't have anything happen to her for the world.' The groom's concern for his young mistress irritated Edward: he knew that he should be as concerned for her himself and he was far more worried because Julia had been in London a fortnight without writing to him. So he left Rivers to shake his head over Harriet and went back to Woodrington and found the promised letter from Julia there, but only to tell him that the Viscount had made his offer and she had asked for a few weeks in which to consider it.

As he read it the last thought of Harriet went from Edward's mind. He decided to leave for London that afternoon, and when Liz tried to stop him they had one of their rare quarrels.

'When,' she asked him, 'are you going to come to your senses over Julia Sodon?'

'If you mean by that, when am I going to stop loving her, I would reply never.'

'Oh!' She was on the verge of tears. 'You are absolutely besotted about her. You will not see that she is as determined to win a title as her parents are on winning one for her. She does not care a straw for you, Edward.'

He smiled maddeningly. 'Why then has she asked for time in which to consider Crowley's offer?'

'She may be after bigger game.'

'Bigger game!' His eyes flashed dangerously. 'I did not think you would stoop to such vulgarity, Liz!'

'It is because I am at my wits' end to know how to prevent you breaking your heart over that young woman,' said Liz, her voice breaking. 'I was at school with her in Bath and I know her to be cold-hearted, selfish and scheming. She is a flirt too ... Why she used to flirt with our poor little dancing master until he did not know if he was teaching the Gavotte or the Cotillion.'

'Be silent, Liz!' He caught her arm in a grip that hurt. 'Or else, much as I love you, I swear I'll never speak to you again.' He thought of the meetings at the old nurse's cottage and Julia's promises from the safety and surety of his arms. He was a little disconcerted when his sister seemed to read his thoughts.

'Thank Heaven you are not having to meet her now at that horrible little cottage,' she said.

'Amen to that,' he replied gravely. 'I hate subterfuge as much as you do, and especially where Julia is concerned. But her letter can only be construed as a cry for help, which I shall answer.'

'You intend to go to London then?'

'At once.'

'Oh Edward!' She sighed. 'Then go you must, my poor brother.'

They parted with grief on her side and resentment on his, and after he had gone she sat down and wept for him. Humphrey Staveley coming in from a morning ride round his fields, was horrified to find her in tears.

'My love, what has happened?' he cried. 'This is unlike you. Is one of the children ill?'

'It is Edward.' She told him about Julia's letter, and tried to find comfort when he took her brother's view.

'If the girl meant to have Crowley she would not have hesitated. She would have had him at once. He's a rich prize in the marriage market, Liz.'

'Not as rich as his father,' she said, drying her eyes.

'His father?' He was incredulous. 'You are not thinking

that she is setting her cap at the Marquis, Liz? Why, he is as old as her father!'

'I daresay, but he is a widower, with ten times the looks and vigour of his milksop son, in spite of his age. And where the Viscount has to wait for his father to allot him the house where he and his bride can live, the Marquis has five places, all equally beautiful, in which Julia can reign supreme.'

'I cannot believe that the Marquis would consider her, nor she him.'

'Can you not? It has been in my mind ever since I met them out riding together one day not so long ago. Julia was careful to explain how they had met by chance ... but I saw the way his eyes rested on her ... and how she looked at him. He is not much above fifty, Humphrey. Your Uncle Joshua married for the third time at that age and had three healthy sons ...'

Her husband said nothing for a moment and then he gave a sudden snort of laughter. 'What a march he would steal on all those others!' he said smiling. 'If it should be true ...'

'All those others?' She stared. 'Humphrey, are you telling me that Julia has ... many lovers?'

'That I cannot answer, but if the gossip one has heard after the ladies have left the dining-table has a grain of truth in it, Edward was not the only one she met at the cottage!' He dropped a kiss on his wife's wrinkled brow. 'There, don't look so upset. Edward will burn his fingers like the rest, but he is not a fool. He will find her out and in time he will recover.'

Liz thought that Edward was determined not to find Julia out, but when she said so her husband only laughed. Love had come to Edward Beauregard later in life than most, and it had taken him hard, but Humphrey Staveley had enough regard for his brother-in-law's good sense to think that he would get over it and speedily.

Edward in the meantime posted to London with only one thought in his mind, to rescue Julia from her persecutors, and during the days that followed he was more assiduous than he had ever been in his life to call on those ladies of his acquaintance who were launching their daughters on the London Season and the marriage market. Never had he been so eager to accept invitations to balls and dinners, never had he been so anxious to ride in the Park, but at first his efforts seemed in vain because wherever he went he found that Julia was so hedged about that he could scarcely come near her. At last however he happened to be near her at a ball when she dropped her fan. He picked it up quickly and restored it to her: she opened it and thanked him and for a long moment their eyes met. And then from behind the fan she said softly, 'Do you ever ride in the Park in the early morning, Mr. Beauregard? Or do these late hours keep you in bed?' The softly spoken words and the glance that accompanied them were invitation enough. Edward went back to his lodgings with his heart aflame and a few hours later, at seven o'clock on a summer's morning, he was out in the Park waiting for her as eagerly and trustingly as he had waited in the cottage in the Weald.

She did not come until eight, and the Marquis was with her, evidently anxious to guard his son's interests in the lady's fortune, thought the chagrined Edward. They exchanged greetings with cool civility and the beautiful Miss Sodon and her companion rode on. Edward did not give up however: the next morning he was there again, waiting under the trees, but this time she did not appear.

He did not know until later, when the whole world knew it, that she had married the Marquis at eight o'clock that morning and the couple had left immediately after the ceremony for Northamptonshire.

Half an hour after he had heard the news Edward was

on his way to Norfolk, and he did not return to Woodrington until many weeks had passed.

*   *   *

On the day after her brother left Woodrington Liz called on Harriet to apologise for his desertion. 'His mind is so full of his precious Julia that he never even remembered to send his apologies,' she said. 'But your riding lessons shall not stop, Harriet. Let us lend you a horse for Rivers.'

Harriet begged her cousin to think no more about it. 'I shall take Mamma out more frequently in the chaise,' she said. 'Which will be all to the good. When do you think Edward will return?'

Liz sighed and said she could not tell. 'But in his absence will you please look on Humphrey and myself as your mentors, should you need advice or help in any difficulty? May I have your promise there, Harriet? I shall be really miserable if you refuse.'

Harriet said that she would be glad of their help and Liz took her departure in a happier frame of mind, leaving her young cousin to ponder on what love will do even to a sensible man like Edward, and to think wistfully of the advantages that the former Miss Sodon had enjoyed.

And then in the way of an English summer, after weeks when cloudless skies encouraged everyone to think there would be no more rain, there came a spell of thunderstorms, and hailstones as big as marbles deluged the land, spoiling the hay and laying the young crops low, and slashing the Manor roses to pieces.

Mrs. Tycherley lay quaking in her bed at night, regretting the gaslit streets of London. When there was no moon the nights in the country could be very dark indeed, and in Gale Street there had been at least a glimmer of gaslight from the street outside to penetrate the shutter cracks. But here in Beauregard the darkness was like black velvet, pressing about her behind her bed curtains. She alternated between drawing the blankets over her face, preferring to suffocate than listen for the hooting of owls in the trees, and the creaking of boards and stealthy sounds within as the old house timbers dried and shifted, and taking her candle and making her trembling way to the passage outside her room, there to stand quaking until her courage deserted her and she fled back to her room, to find comfort in her smelling bottle, while Harriet slept on undisturbed.

Her slumbers were unbroken by claps of thunder, and no wakeful moments came for her to give rein to her imagination. This was not to say however that as the days went by without Edward, she did not miss him more than she cared to admit, and she even expressed an anxious hope at one time to his sister that he would not do anything foolish. In *True and False Love* the hero had put an end to himself, when his sweetheart married another.

When she mentioned this horrific possibility, however, Mrs. Staveley only laughed and said that she did not think Edward would have time to pity himself overmuch.

'He has neglected his place in Norfolk so shamefully over the past few years that he will have enough to keep his mind occupied for weeks to come,' she said, and went on, 'I can tell you exactly the moods that will take him, in their correct order, because I know him so well. First there will be anger, because of the way he has been treated, and his housekeeper will become almost demented because nothing she can do will please him. Then there will be a determination to forget, and this will not be quite so easy to achieve, and his housekeeper will be expected to provide large dinners for all his Norfolk friends at a moment's notice. And finally he will experience a hearty dislike for all women, and because he is over thirty and Julia was his first love, I fear this may last for some time. Nothing in petticoats will be tolerated during this period, and even the housemaids will be allowed in on sufferance. Poor Edward! I do indeed trust that he may not become a misanthrope!'

Harriet said that she hoped so too, but in the mean-time there were young people at Chowton to distract her thoughts. They, and their friends the Cossetts at Woodrington Rectory, welcomed her with delight into their noisy, high-spirited circle, and helped her to forget Edward, and to remember instead that she was only a few months older than Maria Furlong.

As the summer advanced there was much talk of the ball that was to be given for Maria in July, and Harriet was secretly amused when Maria learned that she had never had a coming out ball and expressed her sympathy and concern for her friend. She did not explain that it had been difficult to arrange for such festivities in Gale Street.

The storms passed, and the sun came back hotter than before, trying to repair the mischief the rain and hail had made with the hay. Directly it had dried out the farmers lost not a moment in getting out into the meadows, the men scything it in long sure strokes, the women fol-lowing to rake and turn it, and eventually to build it into hay-cocks, the smell of the hay mingling sweetly with that of the wild roses in the hedge rows.

One morning when it was exceptionally warm Har-riet proposed to her Mamma that they should take a walk under the trees as far as the lake.

'It looks deliciously cool down there,' she said, 'and you have never visited the lake. Besides, I would like to explore the Gazebo. It looks charming from the out-side, in spite of its broken column. When Mr. Elkington comes again I will ask him if it would be a very costly matter to have it repaired.' She sighed. 'It is distressing how this question of money keeps coming up to spoil our enjoyment of Beauregard. When we heard we were to have six hundred pounds a year it seemed like all the riches in the world, but Mr. Snuff keeps writing in answer to my various requests to say that it will be "wiser not to embark on it at the present". I am glad that he agreed to young Rivers being employed here though. He is so pleasant and so willing to do all that he can to please. I am sure the gardens look better already for his work.'

They made their way down the path to the lake, where the rains had filled it to overflowing, and the great leaves of the water lilies were pushing up through the weeds that choked the fountain.

'How I would like to have that fountain working again!' said Harriet, charmed afresh by the stone shell and the three cherubs. 'It would look so pretty.'

'The stonework is very chipped,' said Mrs. Tycherley disparagingly. 'A lead one would be better. Lady Piggott had a delightful lead fountain in her garden at Tunbridge Wells.'

Harriet reminded her that her ladyship's fountain had issued directly from an urn. 'It was not at all beautiful, Mamma.'

'You are far too romantic,' said Mrs. Tycherley.

They left the lakeside and approached the Gazebo. The path was almost completely hidden now by the turf that had grown across it, but when they reached the door in the little tower they found that it was open, and moreover it looked as if it had been opened quite recently, because the turf was freshly torn up where it had been pushed back.

The two ladies looked at each other. 'Perhaps Cookson keeps some of his tools here?' Harriet said hopefully. It was a long way to bring a barrow and tools from the potting sheds in the vegetable garden, and Cookson was not a young man. She pushed the door a little wider.

'Pray, my love, do not venture inside!' cried her Mamma in an agitated voice. 'It may not be safe.'

'As the roof has not shifted half an inch during the recent storms I cannot think that it will collapse now!' said Harriet sensibly. 'And I would like to ascend that little iron staircase and look out from the top.'

Mrs. Tycherley begged her to do no such thing, and declared that nothing would induce her to enter the place. 'It is full of dirt and cobwebs,' she said. 'You will get your gown so dirty, Harriet.'

Harriet said that it was only her morning gown and the cobwebs would brush off, and added that she could see from where she stood that the roof was firmly wedged on its seven remaining columns. The little staircase had a handrail and she ascended it boldly to the platform at the top. 'This is charming,' she called down to Mrs. Tycherley who stood below in a highly nervous state at her folly. 'I wish you would come up here, Mamma. You can see such a long way—as far as the mouth of the estuary. I do not wonder at my grandfather building a Gazebo here: there is an uninterrupted view of the whole valley and Beauregard village, and the river running out to sea. I can even see the Coastguard station on the cliff with its flag staff and the semaphore mast.'

Mrs. Tycherley still persisted that she would not set foot in the place, and after a few minutes Harriet gave in to her entreaties to come down again.

'I will have that column mended,' she said. 'And we will bring the Furlongs and the Cossetts down here for picnics. Mrs. Pells will make us cold pies to eat ...'

Mrs. Tycherley said that she did not think the Gazebo would be at all suitable for such an expedition. 'You could not expect ladies to venture so far,' she protested. 'My dear Harriet, I am sure Mrs. Furlong and Lady Mary Cossett would not like it at all.' She put her head round the door however and sniffed. 'I don't know if it is the damp,' she said then, 'or the proximity of the lake, but there is a curious smell here. Do you not notice it, my love?'

Harriet sniffed obligingly and said that she could only smell cobwebs. 'What do you think it is that you smell, Mamma?' she asked.

'I cannot quite make up my mind,' said her Mamma. 'And it may be only my imagination of course ... in fact I do not see what could make me think that I smelt such a thing so far away from the house ... But I thought I smelt brandy, Harriet ...'

Harriet sniffed with more zest and caught a whiff that was enough to tell her that Mrs. Tycherley was not exaggerating. 'Do you suppose some of the men come down here to ... *drink*?' she asked.

'We should never know if they did,' said her Mamma in a trembling voice, her thoughts flying to Tunbridge Wells where her groom and her gardener would never retire to ruined Gazebos for such a purpose. She said she would like to return to the house. A spasm, or at the best a palpitation, appeared to be imminent.

The key was on the outside of the door and Harriet shut and locked it, taking the key out. Then she looked about her and saw a track that had been beaten down through the long grass from the Gazebo door to where a fallen tree trunk overhung the banks of the stream.

'Look, Mamma!' she cried, her face brightening. 'There is the explanation of our intruders! Village boys have been dropping down over the bridge on to that tree trunk and visiting the Gazebo, getting up to mischief in the way village boys have everywhere.' She ventured towards the bank and Mrs. Tycherley hastily caught hold of her dress.

'Pray, my love, take care!' she cried agitatedly.

'The water is shallow just here,' Harriet said, examining the stream carefully. 'But I believe the young rascals have brought a boat up here. Look at these marks, Mamma, where something has been brought to rest against this side, just where the beaten down grass ends! I will tell Rivers, and ask him what he can suggest to stop them.'

They returned to the house and she walked on to the stables, where the groom was busy cleaning Molly's harness. Harriet had come to rely on this surly man for advice since Edward had gone and rather breathlessly she told him of their discoveries down at the Gazebo that morning:

'You must think of something that will stop them, Rivers,' she told him. 'They have been bringing a boat under the bridge. You can see the marks of it on the bank quite plain.'

'Boys will be boys, Miss,' he said cryptically, as he rubbed the leather with his cloth. 'They're allus up to mischief ... And the Manor grounds have been neglected so long, what with Cookson being too old to do much and Mr. Walter never having them touched ... I don't suppose he ventured near that there Gazebo once in a twelvemonth.'

She wondered if he had forgotten that her cousin had been fishing not twenty yards from it when he was drowned, and she said that she did not like to think of the village lads getting into the grounds by any means. least of all by the way they had come. 'It is not safe,' she told him severely. 'They might upset the boat under the bridge and drown themselves. I would not like that to happen.' She gave him the key and he hung it up on a nail in the harness room.

'Of course it might not be boys,' he then said cautiously.

'You mean that poachers might be coming in that way?' she asked incredulously.

'Poachers.' He smiled grimly. 'Aye ... no doubt.'

'Well, they won't frighten me,' said Harriet firmly. 'I

will stop them somehow.' She walked away and he returned to his harness cleaning, whistling softly between his teeth.

The honeysuckle was sweet about the windows of the shabby drawing-room in the midday sun, and a honey bee was searching in the heads of a bowl of roses that she had gathered from the garden that morning, but suddenly the smiling gardens beyond the windows were the gardens of a stranger, hiding secrets, perhaps some of them grim ones. For the first time Harriet wondered if Walter's death had not been as accidental as they had been led to believe. Supposing he had been down there after poachers, and found some of them fishing the stream? He might have protested or threatened them, and been thrown into the lake for his pains. Or he might have been just sitting there, fishing for eels in the weed-grown lake with his back to the bridge and the shadows of a winter afternoon deep about him, when somebody had come silently upstream ... She remembered Mrs. Furlong's words about Walter: the father or brother or sweetheart of some young village woman might have had a hand in his death, and if it were so, who could blame them?

It was a disquieting thought and she wished Edward had been there, with that comforting sanity in his pronouncements that reduced feminine fears to nonsense. But he was not there, and she had to rely on herself, as she had so often done in the past. She drew herself up.

'Poachers!' she said. 'If I catch any of them I'll show them who is master here, Rivers or no Rivers!'

9

Edward Beauregard had shown no sign of returning to Woodrington when the ladies at the Manor had two visitors who put all thoughts of the Gazebo out of Harriet's mind and fixed them indignantly elsewhere.

The first one arrived in a familiar carriage with the Merrington coat of arms on its doors and its coachman and footmen in the livery of the Marquis. A sprightly gentleman alighted and gave his name to Pells as Mr. Quintilian Sprigg, and Harriet's interest as well as her suspicions were aroused when the Marquis's man of business entered the room.

After exchanging greetings and a few remarks on the warm weather he told her that the Marquis was astonished to learn that she had taken up her residence at Beauregard Manor.

With his eyebrows raised quizzically and his smile one of incredulous amusement he went on, 'May one presume that it is to be only a temporary stay, however, and that you will be putting the property up for sale almost immediately?'

Harriet repressed an indignant enquiry as to what business it was of the Marquis or Mr. Quintilian Sprigg whether she stayed in her property or not, and said calmly that she had not made up her mind.

'Not made up your mind?' He seemed at a loss for words. 'But my dear young lady, surely you do not intend to live in this out of the way spot for the rest of your life? It would be quite impossible for two ladies like yourselves to spend a winter here alone. It would not be safe.'

'When I have spent a winter here I may be able to

speak with more authority on that subject,' said Harriet, determined not to show her resentment at his manner. 'My grandfather lived here for a number of years, and my great-grandfather before him. In fact my mother's family has resided in safety at Beauregard Manor almost as long I believe as his lordship's family has lived at Merrington Castle, and considerably longer than his father-in-law, Mr. Sodon, has resided at Buldrayling.' She smiled with a slight touch of contempt at the astonished lawyer and added that the Beauregards had always been noted for their obstinacy. 'And I, Mr. Sprigg, am as obstinate as any of them in my determination not to be hurried.'

Mr. Sprigg thought that such a form of obstinacy in this youngest Beauregard was not of a kind that would recommend itself to the Marquis, whose marriage to the beautiful Miss Sodon had made him impatient to heap presents upon his bride, the latest being the house and land of Beauregard.

'The late Mr. Walter Beauregard,' he began with an expression of distaste, 'was a gentleman of odd tastes ...'

'Thank you, I am perfectly aware of it,' said Harriet, wondering how long she could endure his impertinence. 'I have been told also that he had peculiar companions, but I do not think any of them will expect to be entertained by me. Fortunately I still have servants here to summon should any visitors prove difficult to dismiss from the Manor.' And here her eyes rested rather strangely upon Mr. Sprigg himself.

His lordship's man of business, aware of the orders that had been given him to secure Beauregard at any cost, tried another angle.

'His lordship is prepared to be generous in his offer for the property, Miss Tycherley,' he said, persuasively. 'He is fully aware that the estate must have been left in considerable financial difficulties. You have only six hundred acres here, besides this house, which is not to everyone's liking. In fact, I should say that scarcely a house of this size and age survives in the county today. Gentlemen who are the owners of such properties have pulled them down long ago and erected much more handsome modern edifices in their place.' He paused, his eyes taking in the threadbare carpet, the rents in the curtains that had been recently mended, the split and faded brocade covers to the chairs that had split again under Harriet's darns. 'The Marquis is prepared to pay twenty pounds an acre for the Beauregard land.'

'I beg your pardon, sir, but I thought the sum mentioned was thirty pounds an acre?' Mrs. Tycherley entered the conversation so suddenly that Mr. Sprigg positively jumped. Up to that moment, except for a slight bow on entering the room, he had regarded the lady as another piece of furniture. He turned to her sharply.

'I believe that such a price may have been mentioned, ma'am,' he admitted.

'And that, of course, was for the land only,' Mrs. Tycherley continued. 'If his lordship wishes to buy this beautiful old house he will have to pay a great deal more than that.' She nodded firmly at Harriet, smiling triumphantly as if she had scored a point, and indeed she may have done so because Mr. Sprigg had opened his mouth to reply, and Harriet was so afraid he would immediately make an offer that would seal the bargain that she stopped him with haste.

'My Mamma and I know little about the prices of land, sir,' she said in a conciliatory voice. 'We would never wish to drive a hard or unfair bargain with anybody. But what the Marquis would or would not offer does not interest me, because at the moment I do not intend to sell either the house or the land.'

Mrs. Tycherley suppressed a sigh. She had been so certain that a dazzling offer would be made, and for a second her dreams had once more soared to a house in Tunbridge

Wells and a position there equal to that of Lady Piggott herself, and now such dreams were once more in the dust. It seemed that Harriet had been right when she said she had inherited the Beauregard obstinacy. Her mother had thrown over her inheritance rather than be thwarted in her desire to marry dearest Alfred, and charming man though he was, his widow had to admit that his financial prospects had never been good ones.

'The house is worthless,' snapped Mr. Sprigg, his impatience getting the better of his manners. 'It should have been pulled down years ago.'

'But I do not see why a house should be pulled down just because it is old,' persisted Harriet. 'King William has not yet given orders for Windsor Castle to be pulled down I believe. Beauregard Manor is a very beautiful old house, Mr. Sprigg, and I have grown deeply attached to it. I do not think I would dream of selling it to a man who intended to pull it down. In fact, the only condition I might consider, if I did decide on selling, would be that the buyer of the property contracted to restore the house to what it was when it was built.'

'But that is impossible!' Mr. Quintilian Sprigg sprang to his feet and began walking about the room. 'Miss Tycherley, you do not know what you are asking.'

'On the contrary, I know exactly what I am asking,' said Harriet with great calmness and smiled at the angry gentleman as he paused in front of her.

'His lordship will never consent!'

'And that is of no consequence to me, sir.'

Things appeared to have reached deadlock, but Mr. Sprigg too had his share of obstinacy.

'Let us look at the thing in a reasonable manner,' he said, sitting down again beside her. 'I am perfectly aware of how the Beauregard estate was left by its late owner, Miss Tycherley. You may be able to live here for a time, but the day will come when it will no longer be possible to pay your servants' wages, and by then it may be too late. And what is Beauregard to you? You have never lived here before this summer: it *can* mean nothing to you. Whereas the land you own separates two large estates, recently united by marriage, and either owner of those estates would be happy to pay you almost anything you cared to ask—within reason. That lady mentioned just now the sum of thirty pounds an acre. Well, let us suppose that such a sum would be considered by his lordship. Eighteen thousand pounds is not a bad fortune for a young lady. Heirs to titles have considered brides with less than that.'

'Yes indeed,' sighed Mrs. Tycherley, who appeared to be taking first one side and then the other in the discussion, 'I remember Lady Piggott—at Tunbridge Wells, Mr. Sprigg—saying that she would be happy if her son, Sir Mark, secured a wife with only ten thousand.'

'At the moment however I *can* pay my servants,' said Harriet crisply. 'And I do not intend to search for a husband, even an heir to a title. So I suggest that you return to your employer if you please, Mr. Sprigg, and tell him that I am quite content with my land and my shabby old house and have no intention of parting with them.' And she rang for Pells to show him out.

He made one last attempt before he left. 'As you are aware the Marquis has only recently married, and he intends Beauregard to be a wedding present for his bride. Perhaps that may influence you, Miss Tycherley, where everything else has failed?'

This consideration was the last to recommend itself to Harriet and she said so in terms that left Mr. Sprigg slightly shaken.

'Of course I know that a certain amount of sympathy has been left for Lord Crowley in the matter,' he admitted. 'But it is not the first time that a lady has preferred a man's father to himself.' He attempted a knowing smile that died swiftly as he met Harriet's eyes.

'Good day, Mr. Sprigg,' she said.

As the carriage moved out of the drive Mrs. Tycherley said she was afraid the Marquis would be very angry.

'He will not be as angry as I am,' said Harriet. She turned to her Mamma impetuously and knelt beside her, taking her hands and looking up into her face. 'Mamma dearest, do not think me unreasonable about this. How could I dream of parting with Beauregard as a wedding gift to the new Marchioness, after the way she treated Edward? Lord Crowley is nothing to me ... If he is such a weak fool as to let his own father steal his bride then he deserves his disappointment. But Edward ... He loved her so much, Mamma ... her treatment of him was cruel ... I would rather the house fell down about our ears than pass into such hands.'

'It was such an excellent offer, my love,' mourned her Mamma. 'Though I do not like his lordship's man of business. He has a mean mouth. You see how he would have offered you only twenty pounds an acre had I not shown him that we were aware that more had been offered ... Ah well,' she added resignedly. 'It is the last we shall hear of it no doubt.'

'I shall be very surprised if it is,' said Harriet wryly. 'There is Mr. Sodon's man of business to come yet. I have the feeling that these two gentlemen will be every bit as obstinate as I can be when it comes to a tussle between us. Neither the Marquis nor Mr. Sodon will be likely to admit that they have been beaten by a woman.'

She was right in thinking that she would not be left alone for long, but it was not Mr. Sodon's man of business who took up the challenge on the fair Julia's behalf. It was Mrs. Sodon in person who came to call on Miss Tycherley and her Mamma.

Mrs. Sodon had not been best pleased when her eldest daughter had slipped out in the clandestine way to marry the Marquis. While realising that she had made a more brilliant match than the one they had planned for her, it had nevertheless upset all her mother's calculations for the summer. Instead of presenting the next girl Mary at a Drawing-Room that June she found it more prudent to remove her to Buldrayling until the amusement and gossip had died down, while her plans for a magnificent wedding at the end of the summer with all the tenants on the estate invited to a dinner in the park had gone for nothing, and her eldest daughter had been married at a simple ceremony that would almost have disgraced a housemaid.

Upon hearing from the new Marchioness that her husband's man of business had failed over the buying of Beauregard Mrs. Sodon set out herself in not the sweetest of tempers to settle the little nobody who had taken up residence at the Manor.

The carriage and the lady were so magnificent that at first Mrs. Tycherley thought the Marquis's mother—the Dowager Marchioness—had come to visit them, and she was almost disappointed when the lady's name was announced.

Mrs. Sodon entered the drawing-room with the air of one who had every right to be there, her manner a mixture of gracious condescension and kindly patronage, her smiles and greeting leaving them in no doubt as to the honour the mother of a Marchioness was doing them in calling upon a mere Miss Tycherley of Beauregard.

'I have heard about you from my daughter the Marchioness,' she said when they were seated, subjecting Harriet to a hard scrutiny that did not miss her shabby morning dress, and passing from there to Mrs. Tycherley's second-best cap. 'She met you the day you arrived here, I believe. What a charming village Beauregard is to be sure! Every time I see it I think how pretty it is. I hope you have been happy during your stay here?'

'Yes, thank you.' Harriet wondered if the past tense in

the question had been deliberate. She also wondered, remembering the short time she had seen Julia, just how she had been able to tell her mother anything at all about her.

'I heard a rumour in the neighbourhood that you intended to make the Manor your permanent home,' went on Mrs. Sodon after a moment. 'I was very much amused when I heard it. "If that is so," I said, "then Miss Tycherley and her Mamma have far more courage than I have. Nothing would induce me to live at Beauregard Manor."'

'Then is it not fortunate, ma'am,' said Harriet, goaded beyond endurance, 'that you will never be asked to do so?'

Mrs. Sodon gave her a sharp glance and decided reluctantly that she was not a young woman to be bullied.

'My dear,' she said with an expression of sympathy that was equally insulting, 'there is no need to pretend with me. Everyone in the county knows about your cousin, and I do not think you can have been surprised to find that you have been shunned since you have been here. It was no matter of surprise to anybody else, I assure you.'

Harriet battled with the desire to have this self-assured patronising lady shown out, and spoke with a composure she was far from feeling.

'It is kind of you to be so concerned on our behalf, ma'am,' she said. 'But you will be pleased to hear that we have made a number of friends in the short time that we have been here. My cousin, Mrs. Staveley in Woodrington, has welcomed us most warmly.'

'Oh Mrs. Staveley!' Mrs. Sodon dismissed Liz with a sniff. 'Well, I suppose she will have sent some of her friends to call on you. She could not very well do otherwise, considering that you are her relative.'

'I daresay her friends may have looked on their visits as duty calls,' agreed Harriet gently. 'But if that is so they have been exceedingly hospitable. We have been returning visits and dining abroad almost continually during the past few weeks, and we are hoping to entertain some of our new friends here tomorrow night. Nobody has seen fit to refuse our invitations, in fact, far from shunning us, all seem to be most anxious to come.'

'Last week we dined with the Furlongs at Chowton,' put in Mrs. Tycherley with pride. 'And a few nights ago with the Cossetts at Woodrington Rectory.'

'Oh the Furlongs!' Mrs. Sodon dismissed them with a contempt she dare not show for Liz. 'The Chowton property is very small, almost as small as Beauregard. Mr. Furlong calls himself Squire, but he comes of farming stock I believe, and no doubt you will meet families of a kind at his house. As to the Cossetts, I know Lady Mary Cossett is an Earl's daughter, but you would never think it to look at her. She is always shabby, and my house-keeper would be ashamed to wear her bonnets, while she thinks of nothing except soup kitchens in the winter and church schools in the summer. She is so easily taken in, poor thing. You will meet nobody of any consequence there, Miss Tycherley.'

'I do not think that I want to meet people of conse-quence, ma'am,' said Harriet meekly. 'I only wish to live at peace with my neighbours.'

Mrs. Sodon looked at her thoughtfully. She was begin-ning to understand why Mr. Sprigg had found his mission difficult: she did not think Harriet was obstinate though. She merely concluded that she was determined to get as much as she possibly could for her wretched property. She began again, in a smooth tone that tried to be soothing.

'You are a very clever young woman, Miss Tycherley. Oh yes you are. It is no good denying it. I am sure your dear Mamma will agree with me. I have always admired clever women, and I have no patience with men who ad-mire women solely for their looks. The truth is of course that they are frightened if we show any superiority of in-tellect to themselves.' She smiled ingratiatingly. 'I will put my cards on the table. This morning I had a heart-broken letter from my daughter begging me to persuade you to sell your little property to the Marquis. Julia has set her heart on having it for a wedding present, and the Marquis has set his heart on giving it to her. In short, you are standing in the way of the happiness of two people, Miss Tycherley. Do you think it is right ... or kind ... ? It is the first time my darling child has been refused anything that she has set her heart on.'

'Do her good,' said Mrs. Tycherley with her usual unexpected suddenness.

'I beg your pardon?' said Mrs. Sodon, bridling.

'She sounds deplorably spoiled, ma'am,' said Mrs. Tycherley, pursing her lips and looking very disapproving.

'Well, perhaps she *is* a little bit spoiled,' agreed Mrs. Sodon. 'But it is difficult not to spoil a girl with such exceptional qualities.' She turned to Harriet. 'Come now, Miss Tycherley, what do you want for your land? Twenty thousand pounds? Thirty? The Marquis is a rich man, and the property can mean nothing to you. You are a newcomer here ... an upstart almost ... You cannot refuse to sell out of sheer perverseness. You have far too much sense for that.'

Thirty thousand pounds ... It was a tempting offer, and if it had been anyone else but Julia who had wanted Beauregard Harriet might have hesitated. But she could not forget how she had treated Edward, and she remembered in time that the Manor had been her mother's home. While she tried to put her refusal into words that might not sound too brusque Mrs. Tycherley sailed once more into the attack, like a small frigate turning her guns on a man of war. 'Naboth,' she said. 'Naboth's vineyard ... That is what it is. The Rector preached a sermon on it last Sunday. I will not say that your daughter is a Jezebel, ma'am, but I wonder that you have the effrontery to come here to Beauregard and call Harriet an upstart to her face. The only upstarts *I* know in the county are certain people who have made fortunes in trade, and set themselves up to be country gentlemen, marrying their daughters to those of the nobility who are content to look no further than their purses—more shame to them. The Marquis may receive a hundred thousand pounds with your daughter, ma'am, but if it were three times as much he will have made a bad bargain. In short, although he deserves it for the way he treated his son, I could be sorry for the man.'

Harriet gazed speechlessly at her Mamma, not knowing whether to laugh or to cry, and even as she battled with her rising hysteria Mrs. Sodon was finally routed. Mrs. Tycherley pulled the bell rope and told Pells to show their visitor to her carriage.

'Had I been treated with even common civility, ma'am,' said Mrs. Sodon, crimson faced and gasping, 'I might have extended a hope that we should see you and Miss Tycherley at Buldrayling. That is out of the question.'

Mrs. Tycherley curtsied deeply. 'You may rest assured, ma'am, that we shall not even return your visit,' she said, and only when the lady's carriage had departed did she totter to a chair and ask faintly for her smelling bottle. Harriet put it into her hands and kissed her and then she fled to her room, there to give way to laughter, which swiftly changed to tears however as she thought of Julia and the way she had broken Edward's heart.

10

Dinner at Beauregard on the following day was a great success. Mrs. Pells served an excellent meal, the wines that Pells brought from the cellars were praised by all, and afterwards, while their elders settled down to cards, Harriet and the young Furlongs and Cossetts danced in the ballroom, while Liz played country dances for them on the old pianoforte there. Her husband would never dance when there was a chance of whist.

And if the instrument was out of tune and there were not more than a score of wax candles in the great chandeliers nobody minded, because the gap in the plaster ceiling was not so noticeable, and the windows opened on to the lawns, now cropped short by Mr. Price's obliging sheep. The moon swung up over the trees outside and the Manor came to life with gay voices and laughter and the sound of country dances.

Expeditions were planned for the summer days ahead: Harriet must explore all the local beauty spots, starting with Chowton Beacon. They would picnic there, they said: Maria Furlong and her brother Bertram and young Jeremy Cossett arranged it all, and before they left that night, a day in the following week had been fixed on for the excursion.

Liz refused to be of the party: her children were too small to climb the Beacon, and she preferred to eat her meals comfortably at a table, seated in a chair, but Mrs. Tycherley, Mrs. Furlong and Lady Mary Cossett volunteered to go with them to choose a suitable spot below the Beacon for the picnic hampers.

The day dawned bright and warm and an old Stanhope phaeton was brought out of the Beauregard coach-house for young Rivers to brush and polish before Molly was put into the shafts and they started off down the approach. To Harriet's delight the little mare did not jib at the heavier carriage, but took it with her usual good humour, only pretending to shy at the carrier's cumbersome cart that met them on its way to the carrier's block. The carrier, Adam Treddle, touched his hat respectfully and waited until they had passed before taking his cart on.

'It is the cover to the cart that Molly does not like,' Harriet said, brushing the flies away from the little mare's ears with her whip. 'And I cannot blame her. It is such a big cover: it must look enormous to her.'

'I suppose he is bringing us something from Woodrington,' said Mrs. Tycherley doubtfully. 'But I can never discover what it is that he does bring.' Adam was at the Manor two or three times a week, and as it seemed to be always on the days when they were out she had come to the conclusion that he was a friend of the Pellses and dropped in to refresh himself with Mrs. Pells's homemade wine.

At the gates a small cavalcade of riders were going by, which was so unusual that Harriet looked at them with an interest which the leader returned. He was a good-looking, fair-haired young man in the uniform of a Lieutenant in the Royal Navy, his companions three petty officers, and he thanked her for waiting for them with a smart salute.

'Who was that?' she asked as he disappeared down the lane.

'Lieutenant Wilberforce, Miss,' said Rivers from the back of the carriage. 'He is the new officer in charge of the Coastguards in the barracks on the cliff.'

She asked what the Lieutenant was doing so far inland so early in the morning, and the groom said evasively that he supposed they had been out all night searching for contraband.

Harriet glanced at the peaceful river bed, empty except for herons and the occasional jewelled flash of a kingfisher, and the Lieutenant's activities seemed unnecessary. They turned away from the valley and climbed a hill steeply, descending on the other side into the Weald, with its fields and meadows yellow with buttercups and the sunshine glinting on the church spires of its scattered villages. Their party was waiting for them at Chowton and Maria Furlong joined Harriet in the Stanhope, while Mrs. Tycherley transferred herself to a larger carriage, with Mrs. Furlong, Lady Mary and the servants with the hampers. Harriet could scarcely suppress a smile as she recalled Mrs. Sodon's contempt for Lady Mary's way of dressing: her plain summer dress and chip straw bonnet were simplicity itself that morning, and she remembered how her father had told her that you could always tell a true aristocrat from the way she dressed. Jewels and fine clothes were kept for Drawing-Rooms and State occasions only.

Jeremy Cossett stationed himself on Maria's side of the phaeton, leaving Bertram to ride beside Harriet, and they started off, somewhat ahead of the larger carriage and behind an old-fashioned landau that was packed with young Cossetts and Furlongs. As they left the Hall behind them Harriet asked Maria if she had met Lieutenant Wilberforce, commenting on his good looks.

'Oh my dear, he is a dream!' cried Maria, with a wicked glance at Mr. Cossett. 'All the girls round Woodrington and Chowton are mad about him. He has such a romantic history.'

'I never believe in romantic histories,' said young Cossett sourly. 'There is usually something not quite so romantic behind them.'

Maria asked with a pout and a flash of her dark eyes what there could be that was not romantic about Mr. Wilberforce. 'His family cast him off because he wanted a life of adventure instead of settling down to a hum-drum existence on a country estate. If that isn't romance I'd like to know what is!' she said.

'If he wanted a life of adventure why didn't he stay in the Navy instead of joining the Coastguards?' demanded Jeremy Cossett. 'And having joined it why doesn't he stay in Cuckford instead of riding about Woodrington and making out that he is needed at the Beauregard barracks, where I am sure there is nothing for him to do that his Chief Boatman cannot tackle.'

'I cannot blame him for preferring the Beauregard barracks to Cuckford all the same,' said Bertram, taking the Lieutenant's part. 'The Martello tower down there cannot be at all comfortable, and Cuckford itself is only a collection of fishermen's cottages. Even the church gets flooded when there is a high tide. The new Beauregard barracks are extremely well-furnished—Wilberforce took me over them one day. He has very cosy quarters there.'

'But why have they built a new barracks up there?' asked Harriet, puzzled. 'Does any smuggling go on in Beauregard?'

To her surprise this innocent question was met with a burst of laughter, while even a grim smile appeared for a moment on Rivers's impassive features.

'I would be grateful,' said Harriet with spirit, 'if somebody will explain what it is that I have said that is so amusing.'

'I beg your pardon,' said Bertram, the laughter leaving his face. 'We did not mean to be ill-mannered, but Beauregard has always been looked on as being one of the worst places for such activities on this part of the coast. Everyone knows it.'

'Everyone, it seems, except me!' she said with a small, chagrined smile. Her thoughts went back to the peaceful river and its herons and the kingfisher. 'I suppose the estuary makes such things easy,' she said reflectively, 'but I thought the Coastguards had put it all down?'

'And so they have, Miss Tycherley!' said Jeremy Cossett stoutly. 'Take no notice of Bertram. He is a hundred years behind the times. I believe he thinks the Hawkhurst gang is still active in these parts!'

'I have heard of them from my father,' said Harriet smiling. 'But they were all caught and hanged, weren't they?'

'They would be very old men by this time if they weren't!' laughed Jeremy, and their conversation thereafter became light-hearted and inconsequent as they approached the Beacon, its sunlit slopes cut by the chalky road they were to climb to the top. Ahead of them the younger ones were alighting from the carriage at the stretch of grass where they had planned to meet, a farm gate separating it from the chalky road, and it was not until they were through the gate and Bertram was walking beside her that Harriet let her thoughts go back to the smugglers of Beauregard.

'At the risk of being laughed at again,' she said with her wide sweet smile, 'I would like you to tell me privately if you think there is much of that sort of thing going on in the village there?'

'I should say smuggling goes on round the entire English coast from John o' Groats to Land's End, Miss Tycherley,' he replied promptly. 'My father says there is only one way of stopping it, and that is by lowering the duties on imported goods so that it will no longer be a profitable occupation.'

She asked rather anxiously if there was much violence among the smuggling fraternity these days.

'Very little, so Wilberforce says. These gentry realise that if they persist and are caught they will certainly be transported if not hanged. But there are always a few adventurous spirits who will try to outwit the Coastguards by slipping a cargo into an estuary like Beauregard on a dark night.'

'But do ships come right up into the estuary then?'

'Oh no, they could not do that!' Bertram laughed at her ignorance. 'Do not look so alarmed, Miss Tycherley! All that happens is that French boats come across the Channel and stand far enough out to avoid the curiosity of the Coastguard cutters because they know that our men have no right to challenge a Frenchman, and their hands are virtually tied in that direction. The Frenchman then sinks tubs of spirits out in the bay, or at some spot farther round the cliffs, marking the spot with a bunch of feathers attached to an inflated bladder ... very difficult to see, unless you come on top of it, even by daylight. A bladder is much the same colour as the yellow foam on the waves ... I did come across one once,' he added modestly, 'when I was out in the bay fishing for codling.'

'You mean ... you found some tubs?' asked Harriet breathlessly.

'Oh no, only the bladder marking where they were. And I let it be.' He laughed at her shocked expression.

'But surely you told the Coastguards?' she asked.

'Not me, Miss Tycherley! If they could escape the eyes of our Coastguards thought I, without any ill-will towards the aforesaid jolly tars, then it wasn't my business to draw attention to them.'

She shot a droll glance at him. 'I am beginning to suspect that your sympathies are not entirely in the right direction, Mr. Furlong!'

He laughed again. 'Where is the harm in smuggling in a bit of contraband?' he said lightly. 'In the old days everyone had his own private smuggler—even my grandfather, who was a Justice of the Peace! My father has often told me how he remembers the smuggler coming when he was a little boy. Nobody thought anything of it in those days. Nearly everybody in a village like Beauregard would have been implicated in it at that time, from the lord of the Manor to the Rector and his wife ... But I cannot imagine your present Rector and his sister lending any aid to such things these days, can you?'

'I certainly cannot.' She was forced to laugh too. Miss Midhurst was a lady with very strict ideas on what was right or wrong.

They reached the top and found the younger members of the party there ahead of them, and as the view was not anything new to them the girls had separated to pick flowers, while the boys argued about a ship that had appeared on the horizon and was standing far out in the bay.

'Bertram!' cried one of his younger brothers as he arrived at the top with a slightly breathless Harriet, 'she is a Frenchman, isn't she? Joe here says she's English, but I'm sure she's French.'

'By the set of her sails I'd say she was French,' agreed Bertram after due consideration. 'Yes, I'd say almost certainly she was ...'

Harriet left them to their argument and let her eyes rest on the view with appreciation and pleasure. The Beacon was nearer to the sea than she had thought, and from its top the line of hills sloped gently to the cliff top where the new barracks and its semaphore stood. She could see the whole expanse of the estuary from where she stood, with the yellow sands beyond, and the sea was a smudge of blue stretching out to embrace the horizon and melt into it where it met the sky. A few fishing boats were drawn up under the opposite cliff but except for the ship on the horizon the sea was empty of craft.

She turned away from the shimmering estuary to the far line of hills opposite, misty in the sunshine of the summer day, their soft, olive green slopes outlined against the sky and softened with distance and the summer haze: she felt it to be the loveliest valley in the world, and the thrill of possession came back to her again. At all costs she must keep it: she must never give way to Mr. Snuff's common sense, or to the bribes of the Marquis or Mrs. Sodon.

As Bertram came back to her and spread his coat on a hillock so that she could sit down for a few minutes to admire it all, she asked him how it was that if he had only come on the bladder and feathers by accident out at sea, they could be found by a smuggler's boat on a dark night?

'Well you see, some of the local fishermen may be in the business ... Mind you, I only say may be, because I don't know for certain! Do not ever tell Lieutenant Wilberforce however, because he is new to it and so full of zeal that one does not know what the fellow might feel it his duty to do next! And the fishermen only go out on their legal business of fishing after all ... If they should discover anything unusual then of course they might fix it in their minds so that they could find it again in the dark ... They have spent all their lives on the sea and in the estuary and thus have an advantage over Mr. Wilberforce and his boatmen ... But this is only conjecture, Miss Tycherley. I know nothing ... and I would not care to know anything. If these fishermen earn more in one night than they could get in a month with their fish, and if a few farm labourers earn more in a night by distributing the contraband than my father could pay them in a week, who can blame them?'

'I saw a smuggler's sloop once,' said the schoolboy Cossett who had argued about the ship at sea with Bertram's younger brother. 'She'd been captured off the coast and brought into Rye harbour when I was visiting my uncle there. He took me down to the quay to see her before they broke her up ... She'd got a false bottom where they'd found fifty tubs of spirits hidden, and she'd got hollow yards, and hollow fenders, stuffed with tobacco ... She was a fine ship though. It was a pity they had to destroy her.'

And then his younger brothers and sister came running

up to say that they had been watching the carriages below and the servants were spreading the cloths and unpacking the hampers and that they were starving.

So they left the subject of smuggling behind them on the hill top and descended to the picnic baskets together.

*   *   *

The ball at Chowton was only a fortnight away and Maria had been full of it that day, and as they drove home together at the end of what had been a delightful day, Mrs. Tycherley and Harriet agreed that they now had only one problem to solve, and that was how they were going to buy new dresses suitable for such a grand occasion.

The dresses that had graced Tunbridge Wells had been kept in lavender while they were in London, and had been brought out again to wear in the social life they had been enjoying since they came to Beauregard, and with the aid of lace and muslin sleeves had been quite sufficient for the card parties and small dances they had attended. But both ladies felt it essential to appear in new gowns at the Furlong's ball, and the Woodrington shops were woefully short of good materials.

The only silks they had to offer them were English of poor quality and harsh colours and Mrs. Tycherley sighed for the shops of Regent Street. As they drove home from the picnic, discussing their dresses, her thoughts went back to that delectable London thoroughfare, with its white stuccoed terraces, its colonnade, its white pavement and the smart carriages rolling along the wide street. She thought of the footmen gathering at the shop doors, and the plate glass windows behind which one could see beautiful silk draperies and shawls, festoons of lace, and bonnets straight from Paris.

'Do you remember, my love, how we used to leave Gale Street sometimes for a treat and walk up Regent Street together?' she said wistfully. 'And once, when we felt richer than usual we went into that confectioner's and bought a cake from the cage made of barley sugar in the window?'

'From what I remember, Mamma, the cake looked better than it tasted,' said Harriet.

'And the jewellery in the windows there,' went on Mrs. Tycherley. 'I wish you had some good jewellery to wear, Harriet.'

'I have my mother's miniature, set in pearls,' said Harriet. 'And that is enough.' It was the only thing belonging to Rose Beauregard that she had managed to save from her father's impecuniosity. 'I remember that dreadful man selling puppies by the lamp standard in Regent Street,' she went on wryly. 'I wanted to buy them all— they looked so thin and so eager. I could scarcely bear to leave them there.' She turned to smile at her Mamma. 'We will visit Woodrington again tomorrow and see what we can find,' she said.

But there was no need for such a journey after all. When they arrived back at the Manor it was to find that the carrier had left a parcel for them that morning, and when they opened it they forgot how often they had abused him in delight at its contents.

It contained two dress lengths of silk, one in pearly grey, the other in a delicate shade of green, sixteen yards in each, and some exquisite folds of lace.

'These are French silks,' said Harriet holding the grey against her Mamma and finding it perfect for her. 'And the lace is French too ... They are beautiful, Mamma. But where have they come from and who sent them?'

She dropped the folds she was holding and searched through the wrapping papers in vain for a card or a letter, and when she appealed to Mrs. Pells for information the housekeeper said that she thought it was probably from Mr. Walter's friend in the Customs.

'Ah then, in that case he had to be careful,' said Mrs. Tycherley wisely. 'I know my first husband's friend was very circumspect. He said his superiors were a jealous set of men and would get him into trouble if they could.' She stroked the silks lovingly. 'The sleeves can be as full as we please, Harriet. There need be no contriving about these dresses. How very kind of Mr. Walter's friend! No doubt he had heard we were here.'

'I wish he had sent an account with it,' said Harriet, worried. 'We do not know how much we owe him for it, Mamma.'

Mrs. Tycherley did not think that mattered. 'He may be in the neighbourhood, you know, and intends to call on us,' she said. 'And there is never anything more than the duty cost to pay. And here is my name, Harriet, and yours, clearly marked on the outside in black ink, so there can be no mistake.'

Harriet read the direction: 'missis and mis ticherle Beaurcgard Manor'. 'It is odd that he did not know how to spell Tycherley,' she remarked.

'I have never been able to spell,' said Mrs. Tycherley complacently. 'And neither can I add up figures, unless they are in tens. Sevens and fives and eights and threes defeat me utterly, and it is the same with spelling. My first husband said he thought the English language was the silliest in the world and he never blamed foreigners for not being able to pronounce it, though when you come to think of it, French is not much better.'

She went on talking happily while Harriet planned their dresses. There was no time to lose if they were to be ready in time for Maria Furlong's ball.

11

A few days later when Harriet and Mrs. Tycherley called at the Rectory to thank Miss Midhurst for sending them a sempstress from the village to make their dresses, Lieutenant Wilberforce was at the gate, talking to the Rector.

Dr. Midhurst introduced him and he won their hearts by admiring Molly. She was, he said, the nicest little mare he had seen in years: he had noticed her especially when he saw them setting out from the Manor a few days ago.

'I have not seen you riding her for a little while, Miss Tycherley?' said the Rector smiling, and Harriet replied ruefully that she had been forced to give up her riding while Mr. Beauregard was away in Norfolk.

'I have no second mount for my groom,' she explained and added that she would be glad when her cousin returned. 'I want to see Farmer Price one day soon, and it is easier to ride up the road to his farm than to use a carriage. The ruts are so deep that I am afraid of the wheels getting stuck.'

Mr. Wilberforce, who had been studying her thoughtfully, now broke into conversation by offering himself as an escort, and as she hesitated, taken by surprise and scarcely knowing whether to accept such an offer from a complete stranger, he continued easily, 'You will not find me a novice in the art, I assure you, as so many of our Naval fellows are. I learnt to ride almost as soon as I learnt to walk.'

'It would be an excellent thing!' Mrs. Tycherley was full of enthusiasm. 'You know how you have missed your riding, Harriet my love!'

'But I do not see how Mr. Wilberforce is going to spare the time from his duties,' demurred Harriet, unwilling to commit herself until she had given it more thought. Her eyes met the Lieutenant's handsome ones coolly. 'It is very kind of you to offer, sir, but ...'

'I will not take a "but" of any kind!' he declared gallantly. 'Say no more, Miss Tycherley. My duties will not be neglected, in fact I have been anxious to visit Mr. Price for some time. May I call for you tomorrow morning?'

It was difficult to refuse and Harriet accepted his offer gravely before Molly was turned homewards, stepping out more happily in her familiar chaise than in the larger Stanhope.

'Mr. Wilberforce is a fortunate young man to have obtained a post in the Coastguard Service,' said Mrs. Tycherley. 'Lady Piggott had a young relative who was most anxious to join the Royal Navy, but everyone told him that promotion in peace time was impossible unless he had a friend who was an Admiral, and so he gave up the idea and went into the Church instead.'

Harriet considered Mr. Wilberforce dispassionately. 'Would you call him handsome, Mamma?' she asked.

'Why, Harriet, what a question! Of *course* he is handsome! That golden hair and blue eyes and those classic features ... He has a Grecian nose, I think, unlike Mr. Edward Beauregard whose nose is pure Roman.' She glanced at her young companion archly. 'I thought he seemed to admire you, my love!'

Harriet smiled and did not reply. She felt that Edward's Roman nose was a great deal better than a Grecian one, and she was not at all sure that she admired Mr. Wilberforce at all now that she had been introduced to him. She found in him an easy awareness that his looks made him generally acceptable to the opposite sex, and it irritated her. She wondered who he was and where he came from, and why he had run away to sea, and if, as Jeremy Cossett had suggested, his history was not quite as romantic as he would have everyone believe.

The next day started so cloudy that she hoped the proposed ride would have to be postponed, but the sun broke through and blue sky appeared and spread over the valley, and before very long the handsome Lieutenant appeared, mounted on a brown six year old that had been chosen more for his performance than for his looks.

As they started off together for the farm on the opposite hill Harriet asked the Lieutenant why he wanted to visit Mr. Price. 'Surely you cannot suspect him of harbouring contraband?' she said.

'No,' he said seriously. 'The farm is rather too remote to be of much use in that way, but I have a list of the men who work for him and I would like to question them, in case any have seen anything of a suspicious nature.'

'Now what do you mean by that?' asked Harriet.

He shrugged. 'Parcels of tobacco left under a hedge ... tubs of brandy in a haystack ... in payment for farm horses being used at night. The usual thing.' He smiled in a superior fashion. 'A smuggler has this much in his favour, Miss Tycherley. He pays in kind for what he takes. Therefore if Mr. Price's horses should have been borrowed for a night they will have been paid for in that way.'

'But Mr. Price would never countenance such a thing!'

'Of course he would not ... no farmer of his standing would in these days. But horses could be taken and used without his knowledge.'

'Forgive me for contradicting you, Mr. Wilberforce, but I do not think that is possible.' Harriet was sceptical.

'Well, perhaps it is not,' he agreed. 'But I cannot neglect anything that will lead me to the real culprits.'

'The real culprits?'

'Yes.' They left the lane for the hills, with the farm ahead of them, and made their way towards it across the turf with the sheep scattering as they came. 'Somebody, somewhere,' said Mr. Wilberforce frowning, 'is lending cellars or stables or sheds or barns to house a large quantity of contraband. Every time a French ship appears out at sea we know there is a load coming in, and although sometimes we find it before the smuggling gentry do, more often than not it is too cleverly hidden to be easily found, and it is collected and taken away before we have a chance of locating it. When I came here I was given orders to comb Beauregard valley for such hiding places, but you can see for yourself what the estuary is like. Any number of casks could be hidden in the water and under the reeds.'

'But I am sure you will search until you find them,' said Harriet dryly and he apologised for having bored her with such details.

'I am not at all bored,' she assured him. 'I only wish you could discover that Mr. Sodon is harbouring contraband.'

'The Buldrayling estate is like the Merrington, above suspicion,' he said, taking her more seriously than she had intended. 'No land smuggler could take a load through either of those estates without running into gamekeepers and such fellows on the look out for poachers and thieves. But there are other places ...' He paused a little awkwardly, and Harriet finished the sentence for him.

'Such as Beauregard?' She smiled ruefully. 'I admit that I have no gamekeepers and there may be poachers on my land, though I have not seen any such characters myself. But I have never seen a smuggler either ... at least I don't think I have! But you are at liberty to come and search the Manor any time you wish for your contraband, and when you have finished Pells shall bring you a glass of my cousin Walter's excellent wine—not smuggled, mind, but bought and paid for in the usual way!'

Her light dismissal of his official position in Beauregard encouraged him to dismiss it too, and it was not long before she found herself regretting it. He was a young man, she discovered, who needed no encouragement at all to talk about himself, and it was not long before he had made her acquainted with what Maria Furlong had called his 'romantic' history.

He touched lightly on the large country estate where he had been brought up, and dwelt on how bored he had become with the hunting and shooting that was thought to be the only life for an English gentleman. 'I wanted to see the world,' he told her. 'I was born with an adventurous spirit, Miss Tycherley, and at last, when I was sixteen, I ran away and joined the Royal Navy.'

From there she was given a brief and dazzling sketch of his rapid rise to Midshipman and then Lieutenant, before being offered the post of Chief Officer on the Beauregard Coastguard section. 'I daresay it was because I am an excellent shot,' he added without any pretence at modesty. 'Our head gamekeeper taught me to shoot, and he had nothing but praise for the way I handled a gun. I am not boasting, Miss Tycherley. Some have these gifts and others have not ... Why, some men who are born to the saddle cannot ride at all but sit their mounts like sacks of potatoes to their dying day. And others, with the finest guns in the world for their use, cannot hit a haystack at five yards. I suppose it is because I have a naturally steady eye that I seldom miss a target, however fast it is moving, and that is why, as I said before, I was given command of Beauregard.'

His complacency shocked his companion. Was he too insensitive to realise that he was talking about human targets now, and not pheasants and partridge on a country estate? She asked if he had brothers and sisters and was told that he had been the only child.

'My parents died when I was young,' he explained, 'and I was brought up in my uncle's house.'

'The uncle then had the country house?' she asked.

For a second he hesitated and then he said yes, it was so. 'But whereas to him a country life meant nothing but delight, to me it spelt utter boredom. I wanted something better out of life than that. I needed excitement!'

'And so you ran away,' she finished for him, thankful that they had arrived at last at Mr. Price's farm gates.

The farmer welcomed them both kindly, though he favoured Harriet's companion with an old-fashioned look at first as if he did not know quite what to make of him riding out there in that easy way with the lady of Beauregard Manor.

But when Harriet explained that she could not ride well enough yet to be without an escort and the Lieutenant explained his business his brow cleared and he laughed.

'Mr. Wilberforce, sir,' he said genially, 'come and see my stables for yourself, and if you think anyone could take my horses on the darkest night without my knowledge I am willing for you to come here and try it yourself.' He led the way into the stable-yard, where two large sheep dogs sprang to the end of their chains and shouted their furious dislike of strangers while a flock of guineafowl ran out from a barn, making almost as much noise and keeping it up much longer.

'Dogs can be poisoned or shot,' the farmer said soberly, 'But I defy anybody to get by guinea-fowl. They know a footstep, however soft it may be, and their screams will bring me to that window there with a gun.' He pointed to a back window in the house that overlooked the yard. 'My horses are locked up in their stables at night and they are far too valuable to be used for contraband. No brandy keg would pay for damage done to them, Mr. Wilberforce, and if I found such a thing on my land I'd find out who had put it there before I dumped it in the river.'

The Lieutenant's blue eyes were suddenly sharp. 'And how would you discover who it was that had put it there, Mr. Price?' he asked.

The farmer replied blandly that as he had never found any the question did not arise.

In the meantime Harriet was being regaled with a glass of milk in the farmhouse kitchen, where Mrs. Price was making gooseberry preserve helped, surprisingly enough, by her eldest daughter Letty. It seemed that neither mother nor daughter preferred to sit in the parlour, though a pianoforte could be seen through the open door, and there appeared to be far more maid-servants than at the Manor.

One of the young Prices came in while Harriet was sipping her milk, a lad of sixteen, who had been helping to get the hay in.

'I say, Mother,' he exclaimed, 'what is Wilberforce doing here?' He stopped abashed at seeing Harriet.

'I am afraid I am responsible for bringing Mr. Wilberforce,' she told him and explained why. 'But the Lieutenant did intend to visit your father in any case,' she added.

'He will find nothing to help him here,' said the young Price.

'I hope he will find nothing to help him anywhere in Beauregard,' said Harriet, and seeing the laughter in the lad's eye she laughed too. 'Surely it is right that I should hope that?'

'He is considered a great joke in the village,' said young Price, and his sister said that some would be laughing on the other side of their faces before they had done. 'Mr. Wilberforce is only doing his duty,' she pointed out, and Harriet wondered if Letty was taken with the Lieutenant's good looks.

'And he is a very conscientious young man, so I'm told,' added her mother.

'He may be conscientious, but he is a joke all the same.' Her son dropped his voice. 'I was in the Lobster Pot last afternoon—it is no use pulling that face at me, Mother. It was a hot day and I had been making hay all the morning in the lower meadows, and so I thought I'd have a draught

115

of Dawlish's very good ale to quench my thirst before I came home. And there was the Lieutenant, sitting in the snug, also enjoying a tankard of ale and talking friendly fashion to Dawlish, who was as open as you please. I noticed though and maybe he did too that the Lieutenant's eyes were everywhere, and I could see that the old man was as much amused as I was, because if there were any contraband spirits on the premises it was not likely they'd be labelled as such on the shelves of the snug. We talked of farming and the prospects of getting the hay in, and what my father hoped to get for his wheat, and then Wilberforce got up to go. I'd noticed his eyes had been going from time to time to a large keg that stood in a corner by the hearth, and just before he left he tapped it with his cane and said, "Just as a matter of interest, Dawlish, what have you got in there?"

' "In that keg, sir?" says Dawlish, very surprised. "Why, I'll show you, sir." And he whips off the top. "Cheese, sir," he says. "Dutch cheese, and quite the best I've tasted yet. Some of my customers like a bit of Dutch cheese with their ale. Have a piece, sir." And he wiped the knife he'd been picking his teeth with and cut a bit out of the cheese. His teeth being what they are I was not surprised that the Lieutenant refused his hospitality. "Shame on you, landlord," he says, "for selling Dutch cheese in an English inn. English cheese ought to be good enough for Englishmen." And off he went without another look.'

'What is there so amusing about that?' asked Letty coldly.

'Why nothing, except that after the Lieutenant had gone I said to Dawlish, "Just as a matter of interest," I said, "what *have* you got in that keg under all that cheese?"

' "Why cheese, of course, Master Joe," says Dawlish, but the old rascal winked as he said it and laughed. "Would you like a piece to eat with your ale?"

'I said I would and he gave me a bit cut with a clean knife. "Funny," I said as I tasted it, "it's got a strong taste of tobacco." "Has it really now?" says Dawlish. "That's on account of the old 'uns, you see. They will sit round that keg smoking their penn'orth of baccy of an evening, and nothing takes the taste of baccy like cheese." And he went on polishing his tankards.'

Harriet couldn't help laughing but she felt a little uneasy as she rode back with Mr. Wilberforce to the Manor: young Joe Price had laughed about the tub of cheese, but there was no reason she supposed why it could not have contained cheese right through, from top to bottom? And cheese did take the taste of things ... the cheese that Mrs. Slatterly had served up to them always tasted of onions, with a strong flavouring of gin ...

Mr. Wilberforce was patronisingly appreciative of Mr. Price and told her that in his opinion he was one of the old school of farmers, of whom there were but a few left. 'He looks prosperous too,' he added, with a glance for the well-stocked yards and the neatly kept fences as they made their way out of the farm yard. 'He's got some fine cattle here, and his sheep look healthy. Good grazing land, is this downland. No mutton is finer than Southdown mutton.'

Harriet spared a compassionate look for the fast-growing lambs on the hillside. What a pity it was, she thought, that they had to grow so quickly into mutton.

Mr. Wilberforce however had returned to the absorbing subject of himself by the way of Mr. Price's stock and fences. He knew a great deal about farming, he said, because he had a gift that way too. His gifts, it appeared, were manifold, and she wished he were the most ungifted man on earth. 'I have a keen sense of observation,' he told her.

'I should say that you need it in your present post,' she commented, thinking of the landlord of the Lobster Pot

Inn, and she hurried Molly on towards the Manor.

But when they arrived Mrs. Tycherley was walking in the park and to Harriet's dismay she asked the Lieutenant if he would not come in to sample some of the late Mr. Walter Beauregard's wine. He accepted with alacrity and Harriet left her Mamma to entertain him with the excuse of wishing to change her riding dress. She felt she could not stand much more of the young man's conversation, and she hoped by the time she came downstairs again he would have sampled the wine and departed. But she had reckoned without his tenacity and Mrs. Tycherley's hospitality.

Mrs. Tycherley conducted him to the breakfast parlour and was dismayed when Pells brought in a decanter of Mrs. Pell's home-made mulberry wine instead of the French wine she had promised.

'Is there none of the French wine left?' she asked and the butler told her regretfully that he was afraid it was finished.

'I would have liked you to taste it, Mr. Wilberforce,' said Mrs. Tycherley. 'Harriet's cousin left some very good wine in the cellars here and I am afraid this is a poor substitute.'

The mulberry wine however had been made a couple of years earlier, and was now quite excellent with the taste and colour of Sherry Wine, and the Lieutenant assured her that he could not wish for a better.

'I only wish I could have had as good during the months when I was at sea, ma'am,' he added, and proceeded to tell her the story of his life, interspersed with stories on her side of Lady Piggott's young relative who had wanted to go to sea, and only when she asked if his uncle's country place had been in Buckinghamshire, because Lady Piggott had relatives in that county and might know him, did he switch rather quickly to another grand relation of his who was in a 'position of high authority' in the Port of London

Customs Office and had 'a town house in London'—by which he meant his mother's cousin Sam who was a tally clerk and lived in a small terrace of houses near Tower Hill.

'The Port of London!' Mrs. Tycherley's eyes brightened. 'Now I wonder if your relation will know the late Mr. Walter Beauregard's friend there?' She told him about the gentleman who had supplied Walter with French wines from the Customs Sales. 'I do so wish we knew his name,' she said. 'Because the kind creature sent us a lovely parcel of French silks last week and he did not put his name inside to say who they were from. Harriet was quite worried about it. "After all, Mamma," she said, "we must pay for them. We do not expect them to be a gift!"'

The Lieutenant asked to whom the parcel had been addressed and when they had received it, and having entered these particulars in a small note-book he promised that he would write to his relation and discover if he knew the name of the late Mr. Walter's friend. The thought of Miss Tycherley and her Mamma being indebted to himself for such information was gratifying to his vanity. 'Directly I hear from him I will call upon you again, ma'am,' he said, 'and in the meantime perhaps Miss Tycherley will allow me to take Mr. Edward Beauregard's place as her riding teacher until he returns?'

Mrs. Tycherley said that would be delightful, and when Harriet came downstairs, dismayed to find him still there, her annoyance was increased upon finding what had been said. She had no desire to encourage the young man to accompany her on any more rides over the hills. Moreover when Mrs. Tycherley told her after he had gone that he was going to make enquiries about her late cousin's friend in the Customs Service she was more dismayed still.

'Oh Mamma,' she cried, 'I wish you had not told him about that!'

'But why, my love? It is such an excellent opportunity

. . . Mr. Wilberforce has a relation who is near the top of his profession—if you call the Customs Service a profession, and I suppose you do, because I do not know what else to call it—and he is the very person to discover the gentleman's name.'

'I daresay he is.' But Harriet still looked worried. 'We do not want to get Cousin Walter's friend into trouble though, do we, Mamma?'

'Into trouble? My dearest Harriet, I do not understand you. Customs sales are perfectly legal, there is nothing wrong about them.'

'I know that, Mamma.' It was difficult to explain that as most of Walter's friends appeared to have been peculiar to say the least of it, she found it hard to credit that any of them would act in a straightforward manner. She admitted however that it would be as well to find out the gentleman's name if it were possible.

12

Mr. Wilberforce was not a young man to miss his opportunities, and two days later he was back at the Manor asking Miss Tycherley to ride out with him again, and on the spur of the moment Harriet had to invent a visit for which Molly was wanted in the chaise.

'Then tomorrow?' he said, adding quickly, 'Miss Tycherley you are not going to escape me so easily! I appeal to your Mamma. Do you not think the exercise would be beneficial, ma'am?'

Mrs. Tycherley agreed placidly. 'I am sure she will be pleased to ride with you tomorrow, sir,' she said.

So Harriet was forced to accept for the next day, if

somewhat ungraciously, making up her mind that it would be the last occasion when she would ride with the Lieutenant, but here she underestimated the young man's determination, which was equal to her own. The nights were moonlit and there was little to be done after the hours of dark that his Chief Boatman could not do equally well without him, and he intended to take advantage of the daylight hours in which to enjoy himself.

'He is quite odious,' Harriet told her Mamma, but odious or not she had to admit that he could ride well and was an excellent instructor, encouraging her to put Molly at small fences and ditches that she could encompass easily in a way that Edward Beauregard had not permitted her to do.

Mr. Wilberforce was not a perceptive young man, and he was easily able to construe Harriet's interest in her riding as an interest in himself. He argued that, plain as she was, her small estate of Beauregard made her attractive enough for him to think of her seriously, and he was certain that she could be speedily conquered by his own looks and charm.

After their second ride together he saw himself as Squire of Beauregard, with shooting and hunting at his command and a nodding acquaintance with half the county. These notions gave his manner towards his pupil such an air of familiarity that she thought he was allowing his imagination to get the better of what sense he had.

'I believe if I continue these rides he may be stupid enough to think that I am in love with him!' she said crossly.

'And are you, my love?' asked Mrs. Tycherley.

'Mamma! How can you think such a thing? He is common, self-centred and vain, and I cannot endure him, except for teaching me to ride. He is an excellent rider ... but then so are circus performers.'

'He probably wants to marry you,' said Mrs. Tycherley.

'That is exactly what I am afraid of ... not because his heart is involved. There is only one person he loves and that is himself. If he has an eye on me for a wife it is because of my "parcel of land". He did nothing but din into my ears today what a gift he had for managing an estate.'

'He did not say if he lived in Buckinghamshire before he went to sea?'

'No. I have not been able to extract from him where his uncle's estate was situated, and in fact I am beginning to suspect that the uncle never existed, and that his knowledge of country estates and houses may be due to the fact that he was a servant there and ran off with the family silver.'

'Oh come, Harriet, my love, he is not so bad as that. Is he coming tomorrow?'

'No. I said that we were visiting Liz. Poor Liz, she will be sick of the sight of us. But I do want to ask her to beg her brother to come back to Woodrington if only for a few days to buy me another mount for Rivers. Whether I can afford it or not it is essential that I should have a second horse.'

They called on Liz and found her at home and alone and she was highly amused at Harriet's account of Mr. Wilberforce's pursuit.

'He is an ambitious young man,' she said. 'Before you came on the scene, Harriet, he was content to pursue Maria Furlong.'

'Maria is welcome to him!' cried Harriet.

Liz promised to write to her brother. 'You should have taken our offer of a mount for Rivers,' she said smiling. 'And if Edward does not come, then Humphrey shall buy you a mount for your groom. Do not worry about it any more.'

Her letter brought Edward Beauregard back to Woodrington at the end of the following week. He rode out to Beauregard on a cloudy day, the sun shining but weakly above the clouds, and their fringes hiding the tops of the hills. He felt a little conscience-stricken when he thought of his young cousin, whom he had left to battle with her problems alone. At least he should have remembered that she could not ride out without her groom.

He found her walking in the park, ready to take instant flight if his horse should prove to be the familiar brown, but upon recognising his mount and himself upon it, she came out from behind the trees and ran to meet him, her wide smile expressing her delight.

'Oh!' she cried. 'How very glad I am to see you, Edward! Now you can see to the buying of Rivers's mount for me, and then you will be free to go back to Norfolk again.'

'I am flattered,' he said ironically, 'that you are pleased to see me for such an excellent reason, and that you do not wish me to prolong my visit for more personal ones!' He smiled however and she blushed.

'I am sorry,' she said in a vexed tone. 'I did not mean to be discourteous, and from personal considerations too I am delighted to see you. Because if you will buy me another horse you will free me from the persecution of Mr. Wilberforce.'

'Yes,' he said calmly, 'Liz told me he had been tiresome.'

'Tiresome!' Anger sparkled in her eyes. 'Day after day he comes here pestering me to ride out with him, just because I took advantage of his offer to ride with me once to Mr. Price's farm. I have taken Mamma for drives in the chaise nearly every afternoon until there are no more of our acquaintances left for us to call on, I have had a "cold" for a week, but he will not be put off. I am very much afraid that he means to marry me.'

'Well, you must marry someday,' he pointed out.

'But not Mr. Wilberforce!' she cried.

'Why not ...? Well, I suppose Miss Tycherley of Beauregard should look for something better than a Coastguard officer!'

'It isn't because he is a Coastguard officer at all. It is because he is such a *bore* ... with his talk of his "gifts" and his uncle who had a place in the country, though he won't say where! I don't believe a word of it, I think he is an impostor, and I do not want to ride out with him again!'

'In that case it is fortunate that I brought an extra mount with me from Norfolk. He is rather too big for the chaise, but Rivers will be able to manage him, so there will no longer be any need for Mr. Wilberforce's company, unless you desire it.'

'Desire it!' She added after a moment however that she did not wish to rob him of his horses.

'My dear girl, you will not be robbing me. I have half a dozen there in Norfolk eating their heads off and getting fat for lack of exercise. You are welcome to Nero, and I shall take it kindly if you will allow Rivers to exercise him for me with so little trouble on my part.'

He could see that she was relieved that her problem had been solved so easily. 'I don't want to be dependent on you for my rides,' she explained. 'I would not like you to feel bound to ride over to Beauregard every time you come to stay with Liz.'

She made him laugh by telling him about the visits of the Marquis's man of business and Mrs. Sodon, and describing how Mrs. Tycherley had routed them both.

'I have a great admiration for that mamma of yours,' he said as they approached the lake. 'I don't wonder that your father married her. She is quite charming.'

'One never knows what she is going to say next,' said Harriet smiling.

'That is her greatest charm!' He told her how impressed he had been by the cropped lawns round the Manor House and its general air of recovery. 'I noticed too that the Gazebo roof had gained a wooden support,' he added. 'Is that young Rivers's work?'

'Yes. He is a better carpenter than he is a gardener. Do you wish to see the Gazebo?'

'If you will show it to me.' She went with him gladly, pleased as a child to have him there. His very presence made her feel stout-hearted again and safe.

'What more have you got against Wilberforce?' he asked as they made their way down the path.

'He is too familiar,' she complained. 'He brushes Rivers aside when he comes to help me dismount, as if he were master here already!'

'Does he pay you compliments?'

'About my riding do you mean? He could scarcely compliment me on my looks!' She shot him a droll glance. 'Though he did say once that I had a determined chin!'

'Obstinate,' said Mr. Beauregard, studying the chin in question with amused interest.

'I beg your pardon?'

'I said "obstinate" was the word for it, not determined. But that is not to say that it is not an attractive chin. It is in every way an admirable chin. My only fear is that it may get you into difficulties if you are not careful.'

'In what way, Mr. Beauregard?' But the sparkle was back in her eyes and the laughter in her face.

'People with chins like yours do not take kindly to advice. They go their own way and make up their minds and in fact, listen to nobody. It can get them into trouble sometimes.' His eyes met hers drolly. 'And it was Edward before, may I remind you!'

'Edward ...' She repeated his name softly as if she liked the sound of it and then she said more briskly, 'You will be here for the Furlongs' ball tomorrow night. Your sister has arranged it all with Mamma. She is sending a carriage for us so that we can drive to Woodrington in the afternoon, and she and your brother-in-law are taking us with them to the ball. Then Rivers will only have to bring Molly as far as Chowton to fetch us home. If you come with us it will make the family party complete.'

'You have overlooked one thing—that I cannot dance. It is an art I have never been able to master.'

'Oh, but at the Furlongs' there will only be country dancing. Anybody can learn country dancing.'

'You do not begin to understand my limitations in that direction. But do not despair. I will gladly be your escort.' He added wickedly, 'I will watch and admire while you and Mr. Wilberforce lead off after Maria and young Cossett.'

'Mr. Wilberforce?' She was dismayed. 'You do not think that he will be there?'

'I should say it is very likely. The moon will be with us for a night or two yet and I cannot imagine the Lieutenant allowing himself to be left out of such a festivity.'

'Now you have spoilt everything! I was looking forward to it so much, but I do not think I shall go.'

'But you have accepted the invitation!'

'I shall have a cold ...'

'What, another? Are you frightened of a Coastguard officer, with a room full of young men to protect you? And if they fail you will have myself as a substitute! That is not like you, Harriet.'

'No.' She thought of her lovely dress, almost finished, and she smiled. 'But I shall take good care not to be alone with Mr. Wilberforce during the evening all the same.' And then they arrived at the Gazebo and she forgot the tiresome Lieutenant in her pride at the improvements in her little folly.

The wooden post had been fixed only temporarily until the broken column could be built up again, and the building had been cleaned from top to bottom. The grass that surrounded it had been cut, revealing a gravel path leading to the banks of the stream and ending in stone steps to the small landing stage at the water's edge.

'I was surprised to see a landing stage here,' she said, standing beside him to look down at the sluggishly flowing stream. 'You would not think that a boat could have been brought up here from under that bridge, would you? But Cookson said Walter always had a boat moored here, until it fell to pieces.' She added that she had told the old man that she would like to have the lake cleared of its weeds so that the fountain would play again, but he had said it would not be possible.

'I am not surprised.' Edward Beauregard's face was suddenly grim.

'Why?' She was frankly puzzled.

'Well ...' He recovered himself. 'It would be a very costly business, wouldn't it?'

She remembered suddenly that Walter had been found there and she shivered. 'Oh well, it's a project that I must put off to the future, that's all!' she said gaily and led the way back to the Gazebo, where to her chagrin she found that the door was locked. 'I took the key away,' she said ruefully, 'because of the village boys.' She told him of the track that had been beaten down in the long grass between the stream and the Gazebo. 'I think the lads had been drinking brandy there too,' she added gravely. 'Mamma and I both thought we smelt it, among other smells of dust and cobwebs!' She expected him to laugh at her, but he had been listening with interest to what she had to say and he did not seem to think it a laughing matter.

'I will have a look for myself,' he said. 'I daresay the key may be in its usual place.' He put aside the ivy that was growing up the side of the little tower and showed her the key hanging on a nail in the wall beneath it. 'There you are, you see!'

She saw that he was smiling, and a ready explanation occurred to her. 'I expect Cookson put it there, so that he could use the Gazebo as a refuge in a sudden downpour. The lodge has no roof and would afford him no shelter and the poor old man suffers so much from rheumatism.'

He opened the door for her and ascended the iron staircase after her, admiring the view with her and amused and touched by her proprietary air as she proudly pointed out landmarks, such as the church spire and the barracks on the cliff. As they descended Harriet caught sight of an old bundle of sacking that had been tucked away under the stairs.

'Now I know that Cookson has been here,' she said smiling. 'He always puts a sack over his head when it rains!'

Edward accompanied her back to the house and accepted a glass of French wine that Pells produced for him, and after he had gone Mrs. Tycherley asked the butler where the wine had come from.

'I thought there was no more of that wine left, Pells?' she reminded him.

'I thought it wiser not to offer it to Mr. Wilberforce, ma'am,' said Pells with a look that struck Harriet as rather strange.

'Pells, I hope you do not think that Mr. Wilberforce could ever suspect the *Manor* of harbouring contraband?' she cried indignantly.

'There is no knowing, Miss, what a Coastguard officer is capable of thinking,' said Pells smoothly. 'And as for being suspicious, they'd suspect the village pump of pouring out French brandy if they could. They're naturally mean-minded, Miss, and I don't believe in encouraging 'em.'

Harriet found herself so much in accord with this last sentiment that she did not pursue the subject.

Before he left that morning Edward Beauregard had another word with Rivers, when he brought his horse round. 'There's a bundle of sacking in the Gazebo, Rivers,' he said, lowering his voice so that his own groom could not hear. 'It may be concealing something, and on the other hand it may not. Has Molly been used again?'

'No sir ... And anyway, sir, there was a parcel of silk left for the ladies.'

'A parcel of silk? French silk?'

'Yes sir. *They* think it came from Mr. Walter's friend in the King's warehouse in London, sir.'

The two men exchanged glances and there was perfect understanding between them. 'Then possibly it *is* just sacking,' Edward said. 'But if there should happen to be a keg or two under it, for God's sake get rid of them quickly!'

'I will, sir. I'll go down there directly.'

Half-a-guinea changed hands and Edward was turning away when suddenly he remembered something. 'By the way, that fellow you were so concerned about ... Jake or Linnet or whatever his name is. Is he still about the place?'

'I believe Dawlish has taken him on as a cellar man, sir.'

'Has he indeed? Ah well, that may not be a bad thing ... Keep him out of mischief!'

Rivers wished he could feel as sure, and after Mr. Beauregard had gone he made his way down to the Gazebo and unrolled the bundle under the little iron staircase. And as Edward had suspected, there were two small unbroached kegs of French brandy beneath it.

13

Mr. Wilberforce arrived early at the Furlongs' the following night, very smart in his white breeches, his blue
coat with its epaulettes, its Coastguard buttons and the
gold lace on the collar. He was pleased to find that Maria
was to be partnered for the first two dances by Mr. Cossett,
as she had taken second place in his affections since he
met Harriet. He waited impatiently for her arrival, only to
find her hedged about with her Mamma and Liz and her
brother, and when he did force his way through to her
he was told that she had promised the first two dances to
Mr. Bertram Furlong and the next to her cousin.

The green silk gown suited Harriet: it brought out
the green lights in her hazel eyes, and the green ribbon
that Liz had threaded in her hair emphasised the gold
that her mousey thatch had caught from the summer sun.
It had been Mrs. Tycherley's constant complaint that
Harriet so often went out in the Manor grounds without a
hat. 'Even the country women wear sun-bonnets,' she told
her. 'You will get sunstroke, my love.'

'My skull is a thick one,' Harriet said, and it seemed
that her hair had benefited from her crazy whim. Her
cheeks were flushed with excitement that evening, she
laughed constantly with sheer enjoyment, and even Edward spared her a glance of approval from time to time.
She looked what she was, a not unattractive and a very
happy young woman.

His dance with her was a waltz, insisted upon by Maria
because it was frowned upon by her elders. Since Maria
had come home from a year in a school in London she
prided herself on being a fashionable young lady.

'I do not mind if the waltz is a fashionable one in

Royal circles,' Mrs. Furlong told her severely. 'It is an odious dance ... so familiar. I do not like to see a girl with a man's arm around her waist. It is scarcely proper.'

'Oh Mamma!' cried Maria. 'Do not be so old-fashioned!'

'It will not be a happy dance for you, I am afraid,' Edward Beauregard said as he led his young cousin on to the floor. 'As I have told you, I am not gifted in this way. You would have done better to have taken young Wilberforce, who is looking daggers at me this moment. I am certain the waltz can be no strange dance to him.'

'But nothing would induce me to dance it with him, all the same.'

'Why?' He glanced down at her mischievously. 'You do not fancy his arm round your waist, perhaps?'

She made a face at him in the way of the dumpy little Harriet who had first come to Beauregard. 'He is quite familiar enough already,' she said with dignity.

'You will not escape him all the same. You cannot dance with me all the evening.'

'I do not see why not. There is nothing compromising in dancing with one's cousin!'

He laughed, and although he had promised her a poor partner she did not think he was nearly so bad a dancer as he had made himself out to be.

'When did you learn to waltz?' she asked. 'My dancing master in Tunbridge Wells would not let me learn it. I am indebted to Maria for showing me the steps.'

He shrugged and the laughter left his face. 'It was all the rage last winter in London,' he said briefly. 'If one attended London balls one had to know how to dance the waltz.'

She guessed that he had learned it to please his beautiful Julia and she wished she had not asked such a stupid question. He certainly danced it well, and she found it exhilarating to dance it with him, feeling his firm hand on her waist. As he had warned her however, she could not escape Mr. Wilberforce for ever, and she gave him the next dance resignedly, relieved because it was a Cotillion and full of intricate figures that needed concentration and left little time for conversation.

When it was over however it was a very different matter. The Lieutenant had to come to the ball that night with only one purpose: to leave it engaged to Miss Tycherley. It did not occur to him that she could refuse him. He was convinced that he only needed the moment and the opportunity for his future as Squire of Beauregard to be assured.

It was a warm night and the long windows of which Mrs. Furlong was so proud were thrown up, so that the guests could walk out of the ballroom on to the moonlit terrace beyond.

A verandah ran round that side of the house, and it was here that Mr. Wilberforce led his unwilling companion, with such speed that by the time Harriet recovered her breath she found herself at the far end of it, and screened from the rest of the company by a large orange tree in a tub. And no sooner had they reached this seclusion than he seized her hand, told her that he loved her, and asked her to marry him.

She was silent from sheer dismay and this he construed as enough encouragement for him to seize her other hand and declare happily that he would never have dared to speak had she not given him reason for hope during their rides together.

This was too much. Harriet snatched her hands away and backed away from him until the orange tree stopped her retreat.

'Mr. Wilberforce,' she said, 'I am afraid you have been attaching far too much importance to those rides. I am very sorry if I misled you, but it was simply because my cousin was away and I had no second horse for my groom that I was glad to accept your offer as an escort on that first visit to Mr. Price's farm. After that I think you will admit that your companionship was more or less forced upon me. You would not listen to my excuses. I am happy to say though that my cousin has brought a horse from Norfolk for my groom, so that I shall not have to trouble you in that way again.'

The words, simply spoken, held a ring of truth in them that pierced his vanity. He did not try to regain her hands and stood back, his handsome face dark with outrage.

'Do you mean to tell me, Miss Tycherley,' he asked, his voice full of anger and humiliation, 'that you only looked on me as a *groom*?'

'Not as a groom, Mr. Wilberforce.' She tried to defend herself from ungraciousness. 'But I could not ride out on my own, as you were very well aware, and I was very grateful to you for your instruction on my riding, which I found most helpful. Now, however, all that is in the past, and I need only to say that I am honoured by your offer, and sorry that I must refuse it.'

'I see how it is,' he said, smarting. 'I am only a Lieutenant on Coastguard's pay, and you are a fine lady and the owner of Beauregard.' He laughed contemptuously. 'Some people would call it anything but a fine inheritance, but I daresay to those not accustomed to great houses it would appear to be something very wonderful, ruinous and poverty-stricken though it must look to the outside world, with its broken fences and its acres of scrubland. I am only sorry that I troubled you.' And he bowed stiffly and went away, leaving her alone with the orange tree.

It was Liz who found her there a little later, and she was dismayed because she was in tears.

'My dearest Harriet!' She put her arms round her. 'What is the matter? You cannot weep at Maria's ball . . .! What has Mr. Wilberforce done? I saw him come this way with you ...'

'He made me an offer,' said Harriet miserably.

'Made you an offer ...? Oh no!' Liz laughed. 'What did you say?'

'I refused him naturally.'

'Naturally you would do that, my dear. But why are you so upset? You are not regretting your decision I hope?'

'Certainly not ... But he talked about Beauregard ... and the broken fences and the acres of scrubland ... and I know it must look poverty-stricken, as he said ... But he needn't have been quite so rude about it ...'

'Rude? He would have given his eyes to get hold of it, my love. That was why he was rude, because he was disappointed ... Impertinent young man!' Liz was indignant. 'But I blame myself for it ... If I'd taken no refusal but just sent one of our horses over for Rivers, none of this would have happened. He is so wretchedly conceited that the little notice you took of him was sufficient to go to his head. Think no more about it ... Come upstairs to Maria's room and bathe your eyes: we can go in through the side door where nobody will see us, and then you can come down again and forget about him.'

Harriet took her advice, and although she looked rather apprehensively for the Lieutenant when she came downstairs again she was relieved to hear that he had made a plea of business waiting for him at the barracks and had left the house.

Liz in the meantime had sought out her brother to tell him what had occurred.

'I feel responsible for this,' she said in a worried voice. 'I should have sent her a horse for Rivers.'

'My dear Liz,' said her brother carelessly, 'young Wilberforce is not the last fortune hunter that Harriet will have to send about his business, and by the way she has handled him I don't think you need concern yourself about her. She has shown herself to be quite equal to the occasion.' And then Mr. Furlong came up to ask him if he would not like to desert the ball-room for whist, and he retired to the card-room with alacrity.

Liz looked after him with impatience. His attitude towards Harriet was very much that of the young men of the neighbourhood: a slight amusement, touched by a slightly contemptuous indifference. Her looks had not impressed them, even if they were not entirely indifferent to her fortune. But Beauregard was not an attractive property: its very air spelt poverty and ruin.

She sighed a little. 'My poor Harriet!' she thought. 'What will become of you, nice, dumpy, plain little girl that you are ... with that widely honest and very lovely smile ...' The whole world was regarded by Harriet as her friends and her smile embraced them all.

In the card-room Mr. Furlong was talking to a stranger, an elderly man whom he introduced to Edward as Mr. Hawes. He told him that he was staying with a married daughter in Woodrington for a few weeks before going on to visit his son in London. He was a widower, of comfortable means, and a cheerful disposition, and fond of a game of cards. He willingly consented to make a fourth at a table of whist, and while they waited for two others to join them his interest appeared to be focused on the ball-room. Presently, as if to explain it, he said to Edward: 'I am looking for a young man, but he does not appear to be here now. I bumped into him in the doorway as I entered the room and although he showed no sign of knowing me, I recognised him at once.'

'What is he like?' asked Edward smiling.

'A fair-haired young man in a Naval uniform.'

There was only one young man in Naval uniform there that night. 'You must mean Lieutenant Wilberforce,' said Edward. 'He is the officer in charge of the Coastguards here. I am told on excellent authority that he has a romantic history.'

'Indeed?' The other shot him a shrewd glance. 'Do you know him, sir?'

'I have exchanged half a dozen words with him since he arrived in the district, and I am afraid that is the extent of our acquaintance. My sister is the authority that I mentioned to you just now.'

'Ah!' Mr. Hawes was silent for a moment and then he said deliberately, 'His name was not Wilberforce when I last met him.'

'Not Wilberforce ...? Then who is he?'

Again there came that shrewd glance. 'I don't know if I should tell you that ... After all, if he has thrown off the bad habits of his youth and made a fresh start for himself in the Navy I am the last to wish to harm him in any way.'

The two other whist players arrived at their table at that moment and there was no time to say any more. They cut for partners and the game began, but Edward's curiosity remained with him, especially in view of what Liz had told him about the young man's offer to Harriet that evening, and when they had finished the last rubber, before adjourning to the supper room he took Mr. Hawes aside and asked him if he could tell him any more about the Lieutenant.

'I have my reasons for asking,' he said. 'He has formed an attachment for a young cousin of mine and although she has refused him, young girls are romantic creatures, and he may prevail upon her to change her mind.'

'In that case,' Mr. Hawes said after a moment's hesitation, 'I had better tell you what I know ... but I must ask you to treat what I tell you in the utmost confidence.'

Edward promised that he would say nothing, and they made their way out to the verandah, away from the dancers and the card-players.

'He is the son of a Mrs. Woodhams,' Mr. Hawes said

then. 'She has been housekeeper for years to an old friend of mine, a gentleman with a large estate in Buckinghamshire. My friend became very attached to the boy, in fact he almost treated him like a son. He had no children of his own, and the lad grew up to be good-looking and high-spirited, a fearless rider and a first-class shot. It was my friend's intention to bring him up to be his bailiff, and it was to that end that he had him educated. His mother, who had been widowed after only a few years of married life, was an excellent woman and devoted to the boy.'

Here he paused while Edward compared the story with the one that Lieutenant Wilberforce had given the neighbourhood. 'I understand that he ran away to sea?' he said.

'Oh yes, certainly.' But Mr. Hawes looked graver still and shook his head. 'My poor old friend ... he was deceived in him indeed! But grieved as he was by the way he had behaved, for his mother's sake he would not have him followed or apprehended.'

'Did you say ... apprehended, sir?'

'Yes. My old friend assured poor Mrs. Woodhams that he was still convinced that her son was a good lad at heart, and that he would have enough sense to see the error of his ways. He took a lot of the blame on to his own shoulders, for having spoilt the boy and encouraged him to have ideas above his station.'

'But what did young Woodhams do, sir?'

Mr. Hawes frowned. 'I will tell you sir, and I think you will agree that the young man had better treatment than he deserved.'

*   *   *

Mr. Wilberforce left Chowton before Mr. Hawes could openly claim an acquaintance that might have had embarrassing consequences. In that first glance of recognition he knew that his past had overtaken him, and his anger against Harriet increased. He was bitterly disappointed at having lost the Beauregard property, however much he might have abused it to its owner, when it had seemed to be within his grasp. He could have played the country squire there in splendid fashion, and once married to Harriet, no Mr. Hawes on earth would have scared him. His position would have been secure in the county, and nobody would have said a word against him for Harriet's sake, whatever they might have to say about him behind his back.

His anger was still high when he arrived at the barracks, and he answered his Chief Boatman's greeting with a growl.

'Thought you were going to be out tonight,' he said. 'I told you to keep a watch on the valley, moon or no.'

'And so I did, sir,' said the man stoutly. 'And I've come back to report to you on something that I saw down there. You may think it worth looking into and again you may not.'

'Well?' The Lieutenant was impatient. 'What was it, man?'

'It was just getting dusk, and I was coming along that lane alongside the Manor grounds towards the gardener's cottage on the far side of the belt of trees, when I saw old Cookson, the gardener up at the Manor, walking along in front of me with a sack on his back. There was nothing in that, you may say, and indeed I thought nothing of it myself. It was when I overtook him and said "Good evening" that he made me suspicious by nearly dropping the sack, and looking as guilty as if he had been a poacher after the Beauregard rabbits. So I walked on past his cottage, and when I had rounded a bend in the lane I doubled back behind the trees and made my way to the back of the cottage, to find out what it was that he'd got in the sack. I reckoned, d'you see, sir, that if it was something he didn't want anyone to see he'd go round to the back with it. And sure enough that is just what he did. I hadn't been there behind the hedge more than a few minutes before the old creature came hobbling round to the well at the back, and after looking about him carefully he lowered his precious sack into the well, securing it to a nail in the side of the brickwork.'

The man paused and Mr. Wilberforce regarded him with interest, his bad temper leaving him. 'If there were rabbits in the sack he would scarcely keep them in the well,' he commented.

'Just what I thought, sir. So I waited until it was dark and the old man put up his shutters and went to bed, and then I crept out to the well and drew up the sack and opened it. And inside were two of the nicest little kegs of spirits that you could wish to find.'

The Lieutenant whistled. 'Contraband, eh? Did he get it from the Manor?'

'I don't see where else it could have come from, sir, though you wouldn't think those two ladies would be parties to anything of that sort.'

'No, I suppose not.' But Mr. Wilberforce did not seem to be quite sure and his Chief Boatman was encouraged to go on.

'Of course I have heard it said in the village that the late Mr. Walter Beauregard lent the house and grounds for contraband, aye, and made a very good thing of it too. But that may be only gossip put about to hide other things. They're deep in these villages: you can't get to the bottom of things.'

'And sometimes you can reach bottom by accident.' The Lieutenant smiled and rubbed his hands together. He thought of the parcel of silk and the French lace that had trimmed Harriet's green dress that night, and Mrs. Tycherley's talk of Mr. Walter's friend in the Customs, perhaps in order to put him off the scent. Supposing those two ladies had continued where Mr. Walter left off, and were using the Manor for the storage of contraband? They could be making quite a good thing of it one way and another, and it would be easy to stop old Cookson from opening his mouth with a couple of kegs of brandy to warm his old bones through the coming winter. But in doing this they might have over-reached themselves: it was not quite so easy to outwit an officer in the Coast-guards as they would discover before they were much older. Miss Harriet might be sorry then that she had ever compared him to a groom.

The post boy brought him a letter in the morning that sent his exultant spirits up still further: his mother's cousin Sam had searched through the records of past sales from the King's Warehouse in the Port of London over the last ten years, and in none of them could he find a single mention of the names of Beauregard or Tycherley.

Mr. Wilberforce was not surprised and he ordered his horse to be brought round and a posse of men to accompany him to the Manor. He felt he could go there with authority now, and if the two women had nothing to say to him he was fairly certain he would be able to frighten their butler Pells into admitting everything. He was a shifty creature and looked as if he could easily be made to talk.

14

Harriet was astonished to see Lieutenant Wilberforce, accompanied by a small band of his men, riding up the approach to the Manor on the morning after the Fur-longs' ball.

He ignored Pells's statement that Miss Tycherley was unable to see him, and thrusting him aside stalked past him into the drawing-room, and if Harriet had suspected him of being about to renew his offer of the night before she was speedily disillusioned. He bowed stiffly and scarcely apologised for his intrusion.

'I am here on duty, ma'am,' he said, pointedly addressing Mrs. Tycherley.

'On duty, sir?' She was so surprised that it was left to Harriet to ask with some dignity what possible duty could bring the Coastguards to her house.

His glance in her direction was insolent and assured. 'I have reason to believe that the Manor is being used for the storage of contraband,' he said. 'It seems likely that you have a quantity of goods hidden on these premises, and I shall be obliged if you will tell me where they are to be found. Otherwise I shall be forced to do my duty and conduct a search with the aid of my men.'

She caught her breath, flushing scarlet not only at the words but the way in which they were said. 'I don't know from what source you have had such information, sir,' she said quietly. 'I presume you must have had it from somebody. But you are mistaken of course. If there had been any contraband here I would have handed it over to the authorities when I took possession of the house.'

He shrugged, and his smile was so sceptical that her anger mounted. 'I hope you do not suspect that anything could have been stored here since I came to Beauregard?' she said.

'One has to make sure that nothing of that kind has happened, ma'am,' he said smoothly. 'The estuary is a wide one and the Manor is far up the valley and hidden away in trees. I have heard that during Mr. Walter Beauregard's time the cellars in this house were overflowing with French brandy and wines.'

'It is scarcely my concern, sir, what my cousin did.'

'And he bought the wines and brandy from his friend in the Port of London Customs Office,' said Mrs. Tycherley. 'I told you about him, Mr. Wilberforce.'

'The same friend, no doubt, who sent you the parcel of French silk and lace?' said the Lieutenant with an ill-concealed sneer.

'Why yes ...' Mrs. Tycherley looked at Harriet, who came to her quickly and put her hands in hers. The two of them, confronting him thus, mutely accused him of ungentlemanly behaviour and his anger rose.

'It may surprise you to learn, madam,' he said, 'that I heard from my relation in the Port of London Customs Office this morning, and in his letter he has stated positively that in all the bills of sale from the King's Warehouse over the past ten years, there is no mention of anything having been sold or dispatched to any person or persons by the names of Beauregard or Tycherley ... In other words, ma'am, I am forced to the conclusion that Mr. Walter Beauregard's friend there never existed except in the minds of yourself and your daughter.'

It was too much. 'Are you accusing us of lying to you, Mr. Wilberforce?' asked Harriet, her voice like ice. And then as he did not reply, except for a faint smile, she went on, 'The wines were here when we came.'

'But the parcel of silk was not, madam,' he countered swiftly.

'No.' She walked across the room to the bell rope and pulled it, remaining silent until the butler appeared. 'There appears to be some doubt about the parcel of silk and lace that we received a little while ago,' she told him. 'I would like you to bring the wrapping paper and label, just as the carrier brought it from the parcels office in Woodrington. I want Mr. Wilberforce to see it please.'

'Very good, Miss.' Pells retired hastily, but not before the Lieutenant had seen his shifty eyes come round to himself with a furtive air that he liked to think betokened fear. It was easier to bully people when they were afraid of you, and he was not proceeding very far in that direction with Harriet or her Mamma. In fact, they did not seem to be afraid of him at all.

In a few minutes however Pells returned to say that the wrapping paper could not be found and he thought that Cookson had used it for a bonfire. Mr. Wilberforce said disagreeably that he would have been astonished if it had been found.

Harriet drew herself up. 'The Lieutenant is under the impression that we have contraband hidden here at Beauregard,' she told her butler. 'You will please show him and his two men the entire contents of the Manor, Pells. Take them into the attics and the cellars—particularly the cellars—and leave nothing unexplored. Every cupboard is to be opened for their inspection.' She turned to the Lieutenant, her eyes blazing. 'You had better begin on this room, sir. There are two deep cupboards on either side of the fireplace, as no doubt you have observed, and there is a window seat also with a cupboard beneath it. Open them and inspect them and then leave the room.'

Her air of outrage impressed the Lieutenant in spite of himself. If there was nothing at the Manor and he had forced his way in without reason, he supposed that her grand relations at Woodrington would make things uncomfortable for him if they liked to take the trouble. He remembered that Mr. Staveley was a Justice of the Peace, and secretly uneasy now by the lengths to which his anger with Harriet had led him, he made a show of examining the cupboards and left the room behind Pells. But though he left not a corner of the house unsearched from attic to cellar, even the cellars were innocent of any small kegs of spirits or parcels of tobacco or French silks and lace. All there was downstairs was a small cask of French wine, almost empty, and the mulberry wine he had tasted already.

He was returning to the barracks in a somewhat chastened mood when he caught sight of old Cookson, going down the lane ahead of him to his cottage. He dismounted, handing his horse over to one of his men, and walked along beside the old man for a little way, and told him without any beating about the bush, what his Chief Boatman had seen the night before.

'I would like to know if those kegs came from the Manor,' he said.

At first the old man was inclined to bluster, and then he admitted that Rivers had found them under some sacking in the Gazebo and told him to put them on his bonfire.

'But good brandy like that ... I couldn't burn it, sir. It wouldn't seem right ... so I brought it home with me and hid it in the well.' He looked up at the young man resentfully. 'And now I suppose you be going to take it from me.'

'I should do,' said Mr. Wilberforce smiling. 'You know that as well as I do, Cookson. But you can keep it, on one condition: that you say nothing about it to the two ladies at the Manor.'

'Why no, sir, of course I won't.' Cookson beamed with relief. 'We *never* tell the ladies anything like that, sir!'

The Lieutenant was delighted to hear it. 'Have you any idea why those kegs were left in the Gazebo?' he asked. 'Had the little mare up there been used do you think?'

'Oh no, sir. Not again, sir.'

'So she has been used once, has she, since the ladies came to Beauregard?'

Cookson's faded old eyes met the Lieutenant's uneasily. 'I couldn't tell you for sure, sir. I did hear something about it, but I may be wrong. You can't believe all you hear, can you, sir?'

The Lieutenant agreed. 'I expect that's where the parcel of silk came from,' he said smoothly, and was rewarded by another quick glance.

'Oh, so you know about that, sir?'

'Yes, Cookson. We know about that ... But the brandy now ... why was that put into the Gazebo?'

'I couldn't tell you, sir, but if it is going to get the ladies into trouble I'd rather you took it with you.' The old gardener was suddenly distressed. They had reached his cottage and he stopped by the gate. 'I'll fetch it for you at once. I would rather you had it than that.'

'No, no, Cookson, you can keep it.' The Lieutenant clapped him on the shoulder encouragingly. 'And it won't get anybody into trouble either.'

The old man looked after him a little doubtfully however as he went back to his horse and rode away with his men down the lane.

'Dratted Coastguards,' he muttered after them. 'They never leave you alone ... a lot of spies, that's what they are. Worse than the Froggies.' And he went back into his cottage, heartily sorry that he had not burned the wretched brandy on his bonfire. Like Rivers and Edward Beauregard he knew quite well why the brandy had been left in the Gazebo, but he was not going to tell the Lieutenant that. Not with Jake Linnet back in the neighbourhood and him and Dawlish thick as thieves. It wouldn't be safe.

In the meantime Harriet, who had watched Mr. Wilberforce out of sight, took herself off for a walk in the woods to calm her temper.

'I shall not be fit company for you, Mamma, or for anybody else for the next hour or so,' she said, and when Edward called a little later to ask her if she would care for a ride that morning after her late night, he found Mrs. Tycherley alone in the morning-room and anxious to tell him about the Lieutenant's disagreeable visit.

'I am only relieved,' she added in a rather perplexed voice, 'that he did not find anything ... although I cannot think where they have gone.'

'Where what have gone, ma'am?' Edward sat down and studied the puzzled little woman with a surprised interest.

'Why, all those casks,' she said, in a low voice. 'Don't tell anybody, especially Harriet, but I have not been sleeping well since I have been here, and one night soon after we arrived I thought I heard voices under my window. I did not wake Harriet, because she sleeps so soundly, but I got up and went downstairs, quaking in every limb because I am a very timorous mortal—not a bit like Harriet, who is as brave as a lion! I made my way through to the kitchen quarters, and I heard nothing at all suspicious until I reached the cellar door. We had not ventured into the cellars because Pells said they were full of rats ...'

'And did you hear anything?' asked Edward with respect. 'In the cellars?'

'Yes, Mr. Beauregard, I did.'

'Rats, ma'am?'

'No, not rats.' She shook her head. 'Voices, pitched very low and things being moved about ...'

'What did you do?'

'I was suddenly frightened and I am afraid I ran back upstairs to bed. I didn't say anything to Harriet about it. Do you think I should?'

'I am sure you should not. Is that the only thing that happened, Mrs. Tycherley? You said something about casks ...'

'Yes. I kept on wondering, you see, what had been going on in the cellars. It was not likely that Pells would have been there, moving wine casks in the middle of the night. He is an idle fellow at the best of times, and he would not give up his sleep for anything like that I am very sure. So a few days later, one morning when Harriet was out with you and Mrs. Pells was talking to old Cookson in the vegetable garden, and Pells was out in the stable yard gossiping with Rivers, I crept along to the cellar door and I opened it ... Do you know, Mr. Beauregard, it opened so easily and without a sound, almost as if the lock and hinges had been recently oiled? And down there in the cellars, faintly lit by the gratings all round, I saw what looked to be hundreds of little casks, piled round the walls and stacked up to the roof. I stared and stared, unable to believe my eyes, and then I thought I heard somebody coming and I shut the door quickly and hurried back to this room. But again I did not say anything to Harriet ... I hope I did right?' Her pretty blue eyes met his beseechingly. 'You see, we had heard that Walter had been a bad man, and I thought supposing all those casks contained contraband, and supposing they should be found, and Harriet had to leave the Manor ... I don't know what the law is in these matters ... I am never very clear about legal things ... But she does so love the old place and it would break her heart to leave it now ... which was why I was so astonished, and so delighted too, when the Lieutenant found nothing down there this morning ... But all the same ...' She shook her head over her needlework.

'All the same, ma'am?' asked Edward gently, and she met his eyes directly.

'What has happened to it all?' she asked. 'Where have all those casks gone? And who took them and when ...? I feel as if I must have dreamt it ...'

'And that is what I'd go on feeling, if I were you, ma'am,' said Edward. 'It was just a dream ...'

'In broad daylight, sir? All those casks?'

'In broad daylight, ma'am, and all those casks ... The only thing that need concern us is that they are gone. Nothing else matters. Do not think about them again.'

His air of quiet authority took a weight off her mind. 'Very well,' she said smiling. 'I will not.' She held out her hand to him. 'I am *very* glad to have been able to tell you about it, Mr. Beauregard. You have comforted me immensely.'

'And I am glad to have been able to help in so small a way, such a very courageous lady!' And taking her hand he raised it to his lips before going to find Harriet.

He had a little difficulty in discovering her and finally came upon her in the woods, up by the waterfall, her hazel eyes like green thunderclouds.

'Has Mamma told you what happened this morning?' she demanded directly she saw him.

'She has, and I am very sorry that you have been subjected to such annoyance.'

'Annoyance!' She was still indignant. 'Our cousin Walter may have been a bad man, and he may have lowered himself by allowing smuggler friends to store contraband at the Manor—it is likely I suppose that he might have done so, if all one hears about him is true— but what could have made Mr. Wilberforce think that *I* would lend a hand to such practices?'

'I have no idea.'

She glanced at his smiling face suspiciously. 'I believe you have all the same. There is a smugness about you this morning, Edward, that I do not like. Surely *you* do not suspect me of helping smugglers and dreadful people of that sort?'

'The thought never entered my mind.' But he still regarded her with amusement. Who would have thought that she had so much spirit, this quiet little cousin of his? 'Do not upset yourself, child. Nothing was found, and everything was explained, we hope, to Mr. Wilberforce's satisfaction, except for your parcel of silk and lace. But I have no doubt that there is a perfectly reasonable explanation for that too, and it will come to light in time.'

'But there was nothing in the parcel to say who had sent it!' She thought it over and her anger subsided a little. Behind them the waterfall was noisily energetic, splashing down into a pool that widened gradually to join the reed-choked stream on its slow way to the river. 'It was simply addressed to Mamma and me at the Manor,' Harriet said then slowly. 'I do remember this about it though—the person who addressed it did not know how to spell our name.

'Did he not? That is interesting ... And was that the only address, Beauregard Manor? No "Sussex" for instance, or anything that could make you think it came from London?'

'No. Old Adam Treddle brought it in his cart.' She caught sight of the expression on his face and her temper caught fire again. 'Oh!' she cried, almost in tears of rage. 'I do believe that you too think we came upon it dishonestly! Oh, how dare you!' And she began running away from him down the path, taking no notice of his requests for her to stop, so that he was forced to go after her and catch her up, which he did with ease because of the length of his legs.

He caught hold of her arm and shook it, so that she was forced to stand still.

'Harriet!' he said. 'Do not act like a child! Don't you see that I only want to help you? ... You are entirely alone at the Manor, you and your Mamma, and in my opinion it is a very excellent thing that the Lieutenant has shown himself to be suspicious. If Walter did encourage these gentry to use his house for their purposes they won't be inclined to come back now without your knowledge on dark nights during the winter. And anything unusual, like that parcel of silk, should be enquired into just to make sure that you know where it came from.'

'I do not see that anything of the sort is necessary,' she replied obstinately, but she did not try to remove her arm, and in fact when he offered his along the narrow slippery path by the stream she took it and found it comfortingly companionable. 'I do not visit the Lieutenant's lodgings and ask where *his* clothing comes from!' She saw his eyes on her and laughed. 'Well, do I?' she asked.

'I very much hope that you do not,' he replied. 'It would not be very ladylike if you did.'

The lime trees were in flower and the scent of them was heavy about them as they walked on in an odd contentment to the house, and when she asked him to stay to luncheon he did not refuse.

There was a simplicity about her that he found strangely disarming after Julia's sophistry, and Liz had been right about her smile. There was not only generosity but enchantment in it, and for the first time he found Lieutenant Wilberforce tiresome, and was glad that she had been able to see the young man for what he was from the beginning.

He had no doubt that the Lieutenant's visit that morning had been dictated by wounded pride and disappointment, but he was sufficiently disturbed by it to decide that he would prolong his visit to his sister for a little while in case he should be needed at Beauregard.

* * *

A week later one of the sloops that kept watch on that stretch of coast dropped anchor in the bay, and the officer in charge of the section, a retired sea Captain, called up at his subordinate's quarters in the barracks on the cliff.

After he had given his report, Mr. Wilberforce related somewhat ruefully his abortive search of Beauregard Manor. 'I thought we were on to something there,' he said. 'But we drew a blank, and nothing will make that old gardener talk any more than he did.'

'What I find odd about it,' said the Captain thoughtfully, 'is that the ladies have issued no protest at your highhanded action, and neither have Mr. Edward Beauregard and his brother-in-law Mr. Staveley. As Mr. Staveley is a Justice of the Peace I should have expected to find a stiff letter waiting for me here today, asking me to reprimand you for having exceeded your duty.' His eyes went to the sparkling expanse of sea beneath the cliffs outside the Lieutenant's window. 'It may be that the gentlemen may suspect something to be going on at the Manor, and do not wish their female relatives to become involved in it. Or it may be that they all know—the ladies included—exactly what is happening there, and they are prepared to lie low now that you have searched the place and found nothing.'

'Certainly there was nothing there.'

'What is the position of the house? Is it near the road?

'No. There is a ruined lodge, of which only the walls are standing, and there is a sort of folly that they call the Gazebo, where the gardener said he found these two kegs, but it could not hide anything in bulk in a hurry. The cellars up at the house would have been the ideal places, but even they had been recently swept out and cleaned up, and if anything had been there at any time there was not even the circle of a cask left in the dust on the floor.'

'That is a suspicious circumstance in itself.'

'Precisely what I thought, sir.'

'Is there a lake in the grounds?'

'Oh yes, quite a large one, and deep so I am told.'

'You did not examine it at all?'

'There was nothing to see in it but weeds.'

'Ah yes . . . but under the weeds?'

'Why no.' The Lieutenant looked at the older man quickly. 'Do you think then that anything could be hidden there, in full sight of the house?'

'Possibly not. But in case there should be, do not scare your birds. You have looked and found nothing. That is excellent. Now the village will argue, with reason, that you will have done with the Manor, and in order to encourage this feeling of security you should now pay more attention to the opposite side of the valley during the next week or two.'

'But there is nothing there, sir, except the hills and a few clumps of furze and a chalk pit or two. We have rummaged that side thoroughly.'

'Then rummage it again, letting everyone imagine that you are highly suspicious of the hill-side and the chalk pits and the furze.'

'Very well, sir.' But the Lieutenant sounded uncertain and the Captain proceeded with his instructions.

'They will not try anything until the next dark night, when you will put every man you have available to watch the Manor, especially the lake. Are there gamekeepers up there?'

'None, sir.'

'So much the better.' He looked at the plan of the coast that hung on the wall. 'There appears to be a wood here along the south side of the park. Can some of your men hide up there in case of trouble?'

'Certainly they can, but it is too far from the lake to be much good.'

'Sounds travel far on a dark night. Is there a nearer hiding place? What about the lane? It appears to have trees on the Manor side.'

'Oh yes, they could hide there.'

'Then set more men to watch the lane and the stream, but don't let them betray themselves on any account. If they should be discovered and a fight breaks out they must whistle for help from their mates, but I hope it will not happen because it is far more important that they should do nothing except use their ears. They are to take note of the slightest sound, especially the splash of water. If they should hear enough to convince them that a load has been deposited in the lake tell them to leave enough men behind to watch it until it gets light while the others come back here for drag ropes and nets. I think you may find the result rewarding, Lieutenant.' He put his hand on the young man's shoulder. 'I know you will do your best.'

The Lieutenant drew a deep breath. 'You may trust me, sir!' he promised him exultantly.

15

The summer was passing, and down in the Weald the August sun threw lengthening shadows over the harvest fields. From Beauregard village the women and children went out early in the morning to glean from the golden stubble and came back in the twilight with sacks of corn on their backs, which they took to the miller in Woodrington to grind for the winter.

Edward Beauregard came over to take his cousin riding and was glad to hear that the Lieutenant seemed to have made up his mind to leave her alone.

'He is a stupid young man,' she said. 'He has been searching Mr. Price's land this last week, just when they have all been away on the harvest fields.'

'Perhaps that is why he did it,' said Edward frowning. He did not think the Lieutenant to be a stupid young man, whatever else he might be, and he wondered what had been at the back of his search on the other side of the valley.

'He would do much better if he left us all alone and used his eyes for searching the estuary and the river bed and the caves under the cliffs,' said Harriet severely. 'He would be more likely to find contraband there!'

'Perhaps it is as well that he does not then,' said Edward.

She shot a surprised look at him. 'You said that as if your sympathies were with the smugglers!' she protested. 'Are they, Edward?'

He did not reply for a moment and then he said quietly, 'I am inclined to believe that most of the men who take part in the business of smuggling are on the whole a very decent set of fellows. At this time of year there is still plenty of work for the farm labourer and he can earn a wage sufficient to support his wife and family, if not to keep them in luxury. But the winter is not far off when there will be no work on the farms, and then what is he to do? He does not want to starve on parish relief, and neither do the parish officers wish to pay it to him. The alternative is to make money in some other way.'

'And this is the way you would recommend?' Her young voice was so indignant that he laughed.

'I would not recommend it,' he said with a twist to his mouth. 'But there is a great deal of money to be made at it.'

'Money!' she exclaimed scornfully.

'It is a useful commodity,' he reminded her mildly.

She did not reply. His tolerance had shocked her and she could not help thinking how little she really knew about this older cousin of hers. Because he had been kind to her and she had taken it for granted that he thought the same as she did over simple things—such as honesty and integrity and the qualities in which their cousin Walter had been so lacking. But Edward was experienced in the ways of the world and he had learned the lessons it had to teach him as she in her little corner of it could not do, and when later on he hesitated about being able to ride with her the next day she did not show him that she would miss him. She felt it might be a good thing if she rode out alone with Rivers for a day or two so that she could think about Edward more clearly.

'I have one of your horses here,' she told him, trying to make a joke of it. 'You cannot afford to let me have yourself as well. Liz will be quarrelling with me if I take you away from her so often.'

'My brother-in-law is busy with his harvesting,' he explained 'and I have promised to shoot the rabbits in his cornfields.'

'In his cornfields?' She was puzzled until he told her

how the reapers drove the rabbits further and further into the uncut corn until there was no refuge left. 'And then we have them at our mercy,' he said.

She frowned. 'I think you are rather a cruel man, Edward.'

'All gentlemen like killing things, my love,' said her Mamma tolerantly.

Edward said that his brother-in-law gave the rabbits to the harvesters, who were very glad to have them. 'A bit of pork in their vegetable stews is all they taste of meat from one year's end to the next. A rabbit or two adds flavour to the pot.'

She dismissed him coolly to his rabbit killing, and after he had gone she went to her room and cried a little from exasperation and anger with him and with herself. She wished she were older, so that he would respect her more and not treat her as a child, she wished she were beautiful, as Julia Sodon had been beautiful, so that he would have admired her, and she wished she had been rich—if money was what he liked. But she was young and inexperienced in the way of managing men, she was plain and dumpy and nobody would look at her twice, and all she possessed in the world were dilapidated old Beauregard and six hundred scrubby acres.

'But at least nobody can take that from me,' she said, and she looked out of her window at the overgrown garden below and her tears dried and she smiled and her heart lifted. 'Dear Beauregard!' she said. And then she changed her dress, bathed her eyes and went down to join her Mamma.

* * *

The storm came up out of nowhere that night. There was no moon, and Harriet and her Mamma waited until the thunder and lightning had abated before going to bed, but contrary to her usual habit Harriet did not drop asleep the moment her head touched the pillow. She tossed and turned and about midnight she got up and opened her shutters and looked out across the park, thinking about Edward and their ride that day, until suddenly she saw something that drove the thought of him from her head.

Down in the park, in the direction of the Gazebo, a light had flickered suddenly and then disappeared.

She strained her eyes into the darkness and after a moment it came again, this time in the Gazebo itself, before going out.

She closed her shutters, lighted her candle and went through to her Mamma's room. 'Mamma!' she whispered, shaking her gently. 'Wake up! There's somebody in the Gazebo.'

'Casks,' said Mrs. Tycherley sleepily, not best pleased at being disturbed when she had only just dropped off. 'In the cellars. No need to be alarmed, my love. They are all gone now.'

'You are dreaming,' said Harriet, shaking harder. 'It's the Gazebo I'm talking about, not the cellar ...'

Mrs. Tycherley sat up. 'The Gazebo?' she repeated.

'Yes.' Harriet sat down on her bed, candle in hand. 'I saw a light there. It flickered twice and went out, as if it was a signal to somebody. What ought we to do?'

'Do? Why, nothing, my love,' said Mrs. Tycherley with great promptness. 'Put your head under the bedclothes and go to sleep. You don't want to be murdered, Harriet!'

'My dearest Mamma, that is not likely as nobody appears to have broken into the house. But I would like to know what is going on at the Gazebo tonight.'

'What are you going to do?' Mrs. Tycherley regarded her apprehensively from under her frilled night-cap.

'I am going to dress and then I am going to wake Pells,' Harriet said firmly.

'Pells . . .' Mrs. Tycherley nodded. 'Of course. Make him go and see what is going on, Harriet.'

Harriet did not think she would succeed in doing that, but she dressed quickly in a dark dress and shawl and her stoutest slippers, and taking the candle in her hand again she climbed the stairs to the room where the Pells slept.

At first her knock brought no response, and then as she repeated it louder the bed creaked inside the room and the housekeeper came to the door.

'Oh Miss!' she said as she saw Harriet. 'What a turn you gave me. Has your Mamma been taken poorly?'

'No thank you, Mrs. Pells. But I would like Pells to get dressed and come down to the Gazebo with me. I saw a light down there and I think we should find out what is going on.'

'Oh Miss!' Mrs. Pells's face went white. 'Oh I wouldn't do anything like that if I was you. You'll get yourself killed just like poor Mr. Walter . . .' She broke off as the butler joined them, but as Harriet had anticipated he refused to set foot outside the house.

'We couldn't go gallivanting all over the park at this time of night,' he told her. 'It wouldn't be safe, not on a pitch dark night like this. No young lady could do it, and I don't feel it incumbent on me to leave you and your Mamma and Mrs. Pells and them two young girls here alone in the house, with nobody to protect you all.'

'What do you suggest that we should do then?' asked Harriet trying to hide her impatience.

'Why nothing, Miss. The sort of gentry who are down in that there Gazebo would stop at nothing, they wouldn't. A dangerous lot they'd be, Miss, men like them. You go back to bed—you'll be quite safe there. All the doors are barred and the shutters bolted.' And he shut his own door firmly and the bolt shot home, leaving her to wonder what sort of protection he thought he could be to the rest of them in such a situation.

She went back to her room slowly, not at all willing to follow his example. She was wide awake now and very angry and determined to discover who it was who was making free with her Gazebo. Yet if she woke Rivers she might have the same answer, and the obstinacy in her refused to let her go tamely back to bed. She told Mrs. Tycherley that she was going downstairs for a little while.

'Pray be careful, my love,' said her Mamma. 'Don't go down into the cellars whatever you do.'

Harriet said she had no intention of going down into the cellars.

'And do not unlock any of the windows or doors. You never know what might come in.'

She promised that here too she would be careful, and she went away downstairs and after only a moment's hesitation she let herself out of the side door, extinguishing her candle first. She locked the door again on the outside, slipping the key into her pocket.

It was very dark indeed, but she knew if she could find the path by the park railings she could feel her way down to the Gazebo and she stood still for a little while until her eyes became accustomed to the darkness. After a few minutes she was able to discover the park railings but following the path beside it was a slower and more painful progress than she had anticipated. More than once she ran into brambles that scratched her face and tore her ankles, and once an owl flew close to her head, its soundless flight frightening her so much that she nearly screamed.

At last however she was able to see the dim shape of the Gazebo and the gleam of water in the lake. As she paused to listen she imagined she heard soft sounds all round her, and although she tried to dismiss them as being only her fancy, Mrs. Pells's words came back to her with horrid clarity. 'You'll get yourself killed like poor Mr. Walter . . .' Had he too seen a light in the Gazebo one dark night last February and gone down there to investigate? It was not a nice thought, and made her almost inclined to turn back before her grandfather's spirit came to her aid, and she continued on her way.

The door of the Gazebo was slightly open and beyond it she could see the faint glimmer of a dark lantern under the iron staircase. She pushed the door slightly and it creaked, and the next moment it was opened quickly, her wrist was seized and she was pulled inside, the door being kicked to behind her while a dirty hand was clapped over her mouth before she could cry out.

Whoever had treated her thus roughly however was plainly not expecting a woman, and as he recognised her he let out an oath. 'The Tycherley wench!' he said. He took his hand away from her mouth but he did not let go of her wrist. 'What are you doing here this time of night?'

'I might ask the same question of you,' said Harriet indignantly. His face was blacked and whatever clothes he was wearing were covered with a dirty white smock, making recognition impossible. 'Who are you, and what are you doing on my property?'

'*Your* property, is it?' He laughed savagely. 'A Beauregard!'

'My mother was a Beauregard certainly.' She put up her head. 'What has that to do with you?'

'It has this to do with me,' he said his grip on her wrists tightening. 'If I could put an end to every Beauregard in the country I'd do it gladly with my bare hands. Oh, I've seen you driving about the village, looking about you with your head in the air as if you owned every soul in it. But there's not a man, woman or child there that would not spit on the name of Beauregard, that wouldn't be thankful to see an end to the devilish breed.'

It was at this moment that the door was jerked open again and they were joined hastily by another man with a blackened face and similar dirty smock. 'For God's sake lower your voice, Jake,' he whispered. 'You'll have the

Coastguards on us ...' And then he saw Harriet. 'Miss Tycherley! My God, what has brought you down here?'

'I suppose I may walk in my own park?' said Harriet, and was relieved that the man Jake let go of her wrists until she saw him take up his stand behind the newcomer with his back to the door. The thought that he might kill her was deepened when he asked in a whisper what they were going to do with her. 'We can't let her go,' he said sullenly. 'Shall I put her in the lake?'

'Don't be a fool!' The other approached Harriet more gently. I'm sure when Miss Tycherley knows as it's on her account that we are here she won't say nothing to nobody. Will you, my dear?'

'On my account?' Harriet stared at him disbelievingly, but she lowered her voice to a whisper too. If these men were engaged in running contraband she had no desire to be caught with them by any of Mr. Wilberforce's men. 'I don't understand you.'

'Yes, Miss. You see Mr. Beauregard told us to come here and get the stuff.'

'Mr. Beauregard?' Her senses spun. 'Mr. *Edward* Beauregard?'

'There's no other as I know of, Miss.'

'And you say that he told you to come here tonight?' She forgot caution, outrage quivering in her voice, and once more he besought her to speak low, while his companion muttered something about making an end on't and quickly.

'During Mr. Walter's time we was allowed to use the Manor for storing our goods,' continued the other, taking no notice of the odious Jake. 'If we happened to be lucky and landed a big load that we couldn't dispose of right away, the old house was ideal for what we wanted, with that scrubland at the back running up as far as the turnpike. When Mr. Walter died the Manor cellars were choc-a-bloc with goods, as was the lake down here.'

'Did you say ... the lake?' Harriet felt she was taking part in some wild fantastic dream.

'Yes. Miss. There's hundreds of pounds worth of good French brandy strung on ropes under them weeds and rushes. It was allus like that and Mr. Walter did not mind. We gave him what he asked, and for him it was either us or the Jews. Why, if he hadn't worked along of us the Jews would have moved into Beauregard the day he died. But when you came here with your Mamma Mr. Edward sent word we was to clear out all the goods from the Manor, which was only right and proper, not wishing to subject you ladies to any trouble. We're honest men, what never did a ha'porth of harm to nobody and we allus pays for what we has ...'

'Aye, and others has paid too,' muttered Jake, but Harriet paid no attention to him. Her thoughts were with Edward, and she remembered how he had sided with the smugglers the last time they had ridden out together. Had he been in it all the time with Walter? Had the two cousins been partners in this thing, and was that why they quarrelled? Did Walter perhaps demand too much for his share? She put her face in her hands and shuddered. If she could not trust Edward she could trust nobody—her friends, her servants, the village ... That awful man had just said that the villagers hated the Beauregards, and perhaps for a good reason. She raised her head. 'Go on,' she said quietly.

'Well we cleared the cellars in a fortnight, Miss. That was easy. But this here lake was a different matter altogether. Them Coastguards has been all over the valley, day and night, and we daren't try to clear it till the darker nights come. But seeing there was that storm tonight and they seemed to be interested in the far side of the valley we thought we'd have a go. But I think them fellows has got wind of what we are up to because I've had a feeling all along that we're being watched.'

'Then go!' said Harriet urgently. 'Go at once! I do not care if the lake is full of contraband, it must stay where it is tonight, and you and your friends must take yourselves off. If the Coastguards catch you Mr. Wilberforce won't rest until he's had the lot of you transported.' She turned to the door but the man called Jake did not budge.

'You're not letting her go?' he said angrily.

'I am,' said the other. 'And what is more, you are too.'

'Then I'll go along of her—just to see as she doesn't raise an alarm ...'

'You'll do no such thing.'

'Who says not?'

'I say not.' The eyes of the two men met and for a moment Harriet had the odd feeling that her life hung in the balance.

'I don't want anybody to walk with me,' she said, her mouth suddenly dry. 'I can find my way back and I shall not raise an alarm, I promise you.' She was too bitterly ashamed for that.

'Come, Jake, stand away from that door,' said the man who appeared to be her friend. 'We don't want to face a hanging sentence, any of us ... And you, my dear, go back to the Manor as fast as you can, and make no noise about it.'

The door was opened reluctantly and she ran out and made her way back to the house without hindrance, and with less difficulty than when she had started out. Mrs. Tycherley was asleep and she tiptoed through to her own room without waking her. But she did not undress or try to snatch any sleep herself. She sat for a long time in front of her mother's little travelling desk with a sheet of paper in front of her and when it was getting light she wrote a message to Edward Beauregard.

Dear Mr. Beauregard, she wrote with stiff formality, *I must see you before you set out with Mr. Staveley today.*

I will not detain you long. Please come as soon as you receive this.

Yours truly, H. Tycherley.

She went out with it to the stables and roused young Rivers and sent him to the Staveleys with the letter.

'It is urgent,' she told him, her young face white from her sleepless night. 'Tell him I will be obliged if he will come as soon as possible.'

Edward Beauregard was at breakfast, with his sister, when the letter arrived, his brother-in-law having gone off already into the harvest fields. He read the peremptory little note in astonishment. 'What is the meaning of this,' he asked. ' "Dear Mr. Beauregard," and "Yours truly H. Tycherley ..." It was Edward and Harriet before.' He threw it over to Liz to read. 'Can you think of any way in which I have offended the little creature?' he asked.

Liz read the letter with knitted brows. 'Perhaps something happened out there last night,' she said then slowly. 'Let us ask the messenger ...'

Young Rivers was sent for and told them all he knew.

'Pells said Miss Harriet came to wake him last night to tell him that she had seen a light in the Gazebo. She wanted him to go with her to see who was there.'

Brother and sister exchanged horrified glances. 'And did he go?' asked Edward.

'Oh no, sir. You know what Pells is like. He went back to bed, after telling Miss Harriet to do the same. He was afraid that the person who was using the Gazebo wouldn't take kindly to being disturbed, if you take my meaning, sir.'

'I think I do, Harry.' Edward read the terse little note again, frowning. 'What did Miss Harriet do?'

'Well, sir, judging from the scratches on her face and the bruises on her wrists this morning I think she went by herself.' Young Rivers was plainly upset.

'By herself!' Edward did not try to hide his concern. 'If she did such a thing it was sheer madness. They might have killed her!'

'Yes, sir. But once Miss Harriet makes up her mind to a thing, nothing will shift her.'

A country mouse with the spirit of a lion. Edward dismissed Harry Rivers and ordered his horse to be brought round without finishing his breakfast, and in a very few minutes he was on his way to Beauregard.

16

As Edward arrived at the Manor he saw great activity going on in the park. A body of Coastguards, at least twenty strong, were collected by the side of the lake, busy with drag nets and ropes, while others were wading out into the weed-covered water.

It was evident that a search was being conducted and apprehensive of what they might find he quickened his horse's pace a little, and found that the Lieutenant had arrived at the house before him.

Mr. Wilberforce was in the breakfast room where the two ladies were seated at breakfast, sternly questioning Harriet, who took not the slightest notice of him, answering not a word as she calmly went on with her breakfast.

'You will gain no advantage by your obstinacy, Miss Tycherley,' he was saying as Edward entered the room. 'If you will not answer me here, perhaps you will find it easier to reply to the magistrates at Bow Street. For that is where I intend to take you today, madam.'

Here Harriet spoke for the first time since he had burst into the room some little while before. Her hazel eyes left her bread and butter for a moment to meet his fearlessly. 'On what charge, sir?' she asked.

'On the charge of receiving contraband goods and concealing them on your property, madam,' he said. 'My men believe there may be several hundreds of casks of spirits in that lake of yours.'

'Good morning,' said Edward at this juncture, and the Lieutenant swung round, while Mrs. Tycherley greeted him with an exclamation of glad relief. Harriet regarded him as coldly as she had been studying the Lieutenant however, and he found himself nettled by her manner. He had not deserved her peremptory note that morning, any more than he merited this reception. 'I had your message, and I came at once,' he told her reproachfully. 'Young Rivers could tell me nothing except that you had ventured alone into the park last night after having seen a light there.'

'Yes.' She turned her face to him unsmilingly and he was shocked at its pallor, and the ugly scratch that ran across one cheek. 'There was a light in the Gazebo, and I asked Pells to come with me to see who was there. He refused, and so I went by myself.'

'Surely that was rather dangerous?'

'I daresay it was, but I was extremely angry that anyone should be using the Gazebo without my permission, and at that hour.'

'May I remind you, Miss Tycherley,' interposed the Lieutenant at this point, 'that one of my men overheard you talking to a man in the Gazebo as if you knew him ... and that as you parted from him you said that you did not care if the lake was full of contraband, it must stay where it was for the night.'

'Is that true, Harriet?' asked Edward, trying by a gentle note in his voice to win a kind look from her, but the glance she gave him was anything but kind.

'I told him that because he said he thought he was being

watched,' she said coldly. 'There were two men there as it happens, but as they did not tell me their names I do not know who they were. There was a lantern burning under the staircase but their faces were blacked. The man I was speaking to told me that my cousin Walter had allowed the Manor to be used for concealing contraband, but that when I came here ...' She halted abruptly, remembering that it had been Edward who had given orders to the land smugglers of Beauregard, and then went on quickly, 'they knew they must take it away. He said that emptying the cellars had been an easy matter, but there was still a quantity of spirits sunk in the lake, and it was then that he said he thought they were being watched and I told him to leave it where it was and take his friends and go.'

'Thus showing yourself to be in league with the rogues, madam,' cried Mr. Wilberforce triumphantly.

'Scarcely in league with them, sir, as the other man was most anxious to put me in the lake.' She held out her bruised wrists. 'There are the marks of his hands, if you do not believe me. But I was going to write to you, after I had breakfasted this morning, asking you to bring your men to search the lake, as I had reason to believe there might be contraband there. I do not know what else I could have done under the circumstances.'

'It is easy to say that now that everything has been discovered,' said the Lieutenant sceptically. 'You were going to write to me after you had breakfasted, you say, and yet you found time to write to Mr. Beauregard long before then! I should have thought the Coastguard station to be a great deal nearer to the Manor than Woodrington.'

'I wished to see my cousin because I wanted to ask him some questions. I had already made up my mind what to do.'

'And you seriously expect me to believe that you had no notion until last night of what was going on here at the Manor?' The Lieutenant was contemptuous.

'What I expect you to believe, sir, scarcely comes into it,' said Harriet.

'Yet you would still have me think that you have no idea where that mysterious parcel of silk and lace came from, and that they were not meant for a lady who had been as accommodating as the late Mr. Walter Beauregard had been? If there are a quantity of casks in your lake they may represent hundreds of pounds—no small advantage to the owner of such a property as this. I don't really think, Miss Tycherley, that you could have expected so small a return for *them* as another parcel of silk. That was only to reward you for—possibly the use of your little mare one night, or the right of way over your land as far as the turnpike. *That* was the price you paid for your silk and lace, Miss Tycherley, and I am sure you know it as well as I do!'

It was here that Edward Beauregard took the Lieutenant's arm in a firm grip and suggested that he might like to step outside for a moment, so that they could discuss certain matters together.

'The ladies will not escape you,' he added as the young man hesitated. 'I will go bail for that.'

The Lieutenant stepped outside and Mr. Beauregard escorted him to the drive where they would not be overheard. 'If you think you are going to bribe me ...' he began.

'It never entered my head,' said Mr. Beauregard pleasantly. 'All I wished to do was to stop you bullying my cousin by uttering any more empty threats. For one thing you must know as well as I do that you cannot possibly take her to London today. She is a minor, and if there is any question of legal proceedings against her, her lawyer, Mr. Snuff, will represent her in court, so we will say no more about that if you please. I removed you from the house because I do not trust the butler Pells. He is always listening at doors, and he is the sort of blackguard who would not hesitate to blackmail even a young officer in the Coastguard service if he should learn any secrets that he was anxious to conceal.'

'I do not understand you, sir.' But in spite of the Lieutenant's blustering manner Edward caught a gleam of fear in the blue eyes and was content.

'I think you do understand me, Mr. Woodhams,' he said gently.

There was no mistaking the young man's confusion now, though he still tried to bluff it out. 'Woodhams?' he said. 'You are making a mistake, I think ...'

'I met a gentleman at the Furlongs' ball who recognised you,' went on Edward, taking no notice of his protestations. 'He happened to be staying in Woodrington, and when I heard from my sister that night that you had made an offer to my cousin I felt I must ask him—in confidence —what he knew about you. Your own story appeared to be vague: you were an orphan, you said, and you had been brought up by an uncle in a grand country place, and had run away to sea ... That appeared to be innocuous enough.'

'I never made any secret of the fact that I ran away,' interrupted Mr. Wilberforce angrily.

'No. But you did not seem willing to tell anybody where your uncle's country estate had been situated, which seemed a little strange.'

'People are so inquisitive,' complained the Lieutenant, but he was plainly uneasy. 'Why should I tell them all my business?'

'You cannot blame them if they like to know the family history of people who come to live among them, especially if they happen to be young unattached men, who show an interest in the young ladies of the district. The gentleman at the Furlongs' ball told me an interesting story. He said that you were the son of the housekeeper to an old friend of his—a woman by the name of Woodhams. He said that his friend, being wealthy and very much alone in the world, made it his business to have you educated, planning to make you agent for his estate when you were old enough. Unfortunately your natural good looks and good fortune turned your head. You rebelled against the position you held at that time in his house, and you repaid your benefactor by waiting until you were sixteen and then running away to sea.' He waited a moment to see if Mr. Wilberforce had any comment to make, but as he remained silent he continued quietly, 'On the night that you left, the sum of one hundred pounds disappeared from the housekeeper's room.'

The Lieutenant's eyes went quickly to Mr. Beauregard's and then fell away to the park and the group of men busy round the lake, but he did not speak or try to defend himself in any way and Edward went on:

'Mr. Furlong's friend told me that your old patron refused to have you followed or apprehended for the sake of your mother, who was broken-hearted at your behaviour. The only punishment he meted out was one that you could not know about—he altered his will, and instead of leaving you a handsome sum that would have made you independent after his death, he left you nothing.'

'And old Hawes benefited in consequence I suppose!' exclaimed the Lieutenant. 'He never liked me ...' and then he broke off.

'So you did know him?' said Edward. He stopped and faced the young man, studying his face sternly. 'Do you admit the truth of his story?' he asked.

'You cannot know what it was like for me,' cried the Lieutenant desperately. 'To have the servants' contempt and jealousy because I was the old man's favourite ... to have them sneering at me ... and to be patronised by the old man's friends. Never to be on an equal footing with anybody, neither servant nor gentleman ... condescended to by the great ladies because of my looks ... berated by the steward if I dared to slip away and play cards with companions of my own age in the nearest town ... I could not have stayed there. And I did not think it was the old man's money that I took, I thought it was my mother's.'

'It was the money that she kept there for paying the servant-maids and things of that sort.'

'I swear I thought it was hers ... her savings. I intended to repay it, and I left a letter for her telling her what I had done.' He paused and his face twitched. 'I have not thought of it for years, and now this old fool must come from nowhere to ruin me.' His eyes met Edward's despondently. 'I know you will understand. You are like the rest of them, you have had everything ... you do not know what it is like to be at the other end of the scale.'

'Perhaps I understand more than you imagine,' said Edward thinking of Miss Sodon and how humble his own station had appeared in her eyes, and he went on thoughtfully, 'You have made a career for yourself in the Royal Navy, and the past is behind you. Mr. Hawes is the only one who knows your story, and nobody else will hear of it through me. The Royal Navy is an honourable profession though, Lieutenant Wilberforce, and one in which petty revenge and personal scores should play no part. It also has a reputation in England for chivalrous behaviour where women are concerned. Remember that in future.'

The colour came back to the Lieutenant's face and relief was in the glance he shot at his companion. 'What do you wish me to do?' he asked without any bluster however and with a directness that Edward liked. Maybe there was good in the fellow after all: he felt he could afford to give him the benefit of the doubt.

'I would suggest that when you have saved the sum of one hundred pounds you should send it to your mother with a letter telling her that you have changed your name and acquainting her with your progress in the Navy. It is the least you can do after the suffering you have caused her. And in the meantime I shall be obliged if you will join your men in clearing that lake of contraband, and when it is finished, take it and go.'

He turned on his heel and walked back to the house while the Lieutenant, after a hesitating glance as if he wanted to apologise, and then thought better of it, started off across the park.

Mr. Beauregard found the ladies still in the breakfast room, but Harriet was writing a letter with her back to him, and did not turn at his entrance or cease from her task.

'Mr. Wilberforce will do no more now, I think, than clear what casks there are from the lake,' Edward told Mrs. Tycherley. 'If there are as many as he seemed to imagine it may take a few days ... possibly as long as a week. But I do not think you will be troubled by him here. He is not a bad young man, though I think he has been brought up with a wrong idea of his own importance which has forced him into making mistakes. But he will outgrow it in time.'

'Thank you ... We are most grateful to you.' And then as Harriet finished her letter and sealed and addressed it her Mamma added timidly, 'We are indebted to Mr. Beauregard, are we not, my love?'

Harriet got up and turned to face him. Her face was still white, the scratches livid, and there were blue smudges of fatigue under her eyes, which were full of a scornful anger. Never had she looked so plain, and yet she compelled his admiration in a way that no other woman had done.

'You said that you sent for me to ask some questions,' he reminded her gently.

'Yes.' Her voice was hard and angry. 'You knew about it all, did you not? That man told me so last night. The whole village knew that the Manor harboured contraband

... only I was the innocent party, the stool pigeon, the romantic little fool who thought she was coming home! I even imagined that my cousin Walter might have been trying to make amends, that my grandfather might have left instructions to him to leave the estate in that way ... I thought I would find warmth and affection down here in Beauregard, and instead I was thrown, completely ignorant and unaware into the midst of a lot of ruffians. They laughed at me behind my back, as the whole village laughed, hating me all the time because I was a Beauregard.' She laughed with a bitterness he had not heard from her before. 'And I had looked on them as "my" people, Mr. Beauregard ... ! Well, their smuggling days are finished now, and when you next see your friends among them you have my permission to tell them that I have instructed Mr. Snuff to sell Beauregard to the highest bidder. I do not care if it is the Marquis or Mr. Sodon—my interest in it is dead. When Rivers goes to the Post Office in Woodrington today he can ride Molly. Your groom can take Nero back with him when you go. We shall not be requiring him again.'

'Harriet ...' He tried to take her hand but she put it quickly behind her back.

'Don't come near me!' she cried. 'You knew, and yet you said nothing to me. You are as bad as they are ... worse, because you knew that I trusted you. But I shall never trust anyone again ... ever.' Her voice broke, but she controlled it fiercely and went on, 'Please give my regards to your sister and to any other ... ladies ... I have met since we have been here. I will be grateful if you will tell them that as we shall be leaving Beauregard at the end of the next few days Mamma and I will not be receiving visitors. It only remains for me to say goodbye to you and to regret that I cannot express any desire to see you ... or Liz ... or Beauregard again.' She ran out of the room leaving him alone with Mrs. Tycherley.

'I am sorry she has behaved like this.' A tear slipped down Mrs. Tycherley's pretty nose. 'Poor Harriet ... You must excuse her though, because she is very tired this morning, and she is feeling humbled and humiliated by all that has happened ... You must forgive her, Mr. Beauregard!'

'Forgive her?' he said slowly. 'Madam, I hope the time will come when she will be able to forgive me!'

With his groom and Nero behind him, he rode away with scarcely a thought for the small crowd at the lake side and the growing heap of casks, dripping with weeds and water, that was forming a formidable circle in the background. 'Damn Walter!' he thought. 'And damn Uncle Robert ... why did they have to treat her so?'

As he rode on over the hills there was nothing but heaviness in his heart. He kept seeing Harriet at Beauregard, with her wide, enchanting smile, now completely quenched, and her childlike delight in her ramshackle house and barren acres, and the way she had learned to ride, fearlessly ... as fearless as when she went down to the Gazebo last night ... Supposing she had met the same fate as Walter? Supposing they had found her there this morning among the weeds?

He felt suddenly cold, and it seemed as he came down into the Weald that the clouds that were massing on the horizon had taken the gold from the cornfields and the warmth from the sun.

*　　*　　*

From Harriet's window Mrs. Tycherley watched him until he was out of sight. She had expected to find her step-daughter prostrate on her bed, in floods of tears at all that had happened, but instead Harriet was busy turning out her cupboards and throwing the clothes on the bed instead of herself, and she scarcely seemed to hear the words of comfort and encouragement from her Mamma. It was only when Mrs. Tycherley told her that the fountain was playing again that she uttered one terse word of comment. 'Brandy!' she said.

'Oh no, my love, it looks like water from here,' said her Mamma.

'I did not mean that the fountain was sending out streams of brandy,' Harriet explained. 'Even Mr. Sodon, with all his money, will scarcely be likely to use French brandy for such a purpose ... But I expect they have taken the last of the casks from its base and that is why it is playing again.' She took out the green silk dress from her wardrobe, bundled it up and threw it in a corner of the room. 'Mrs. Pells can have that!' she said.

Mrs. Tycherley could bear it no longer. She sat down on the bed among the scattered dresses and took Harriet's hand. 'What are you doing, my love?' she asked.

Harriet looked astonished at the question. 'I am getting ready to pack, Mamma,' she said. 'I have told Pells to have our portmanteaux brought down from the box-room.'

'Packing ... ? But why?'

'Because we are leaving Beauregard, my dearest,' said Harriet smiling rather sadly at her Mamma. 'And ... this ought to rejoice your heart ... ! We are going back to Tunbridge Wells.'

'Tunbridge Wells!' Mrs. Tycherley drew a great breath. 'Oh Harriet, you do not mean that? You are not just saying it to tease me? You cannot really mean that we shall be going back to our dear Tunbridge Wells?'

'I really mean it, Mamma.'

'But you do not like Tunbridge Wells, my love!' Visions were already filling Mrs. Tycherley's mind of a house with stabling and a neat garden ... of furnishing a drawing-room with the new walnut furniture in the delicate shapes so much favoured by the late King George IV ... of card-parties ... and trim maid-servants instead of these willing, clumsy country girls ... and a smiling housekeeper in place of the frowning Mrs. Pells and that dreadful butler. Then she saw the sadness on Harriet's face and put it behind her. 'But why Tunbridge Wells?' she said bravely. 'Bath or Cheltenham would be just as nice ...'

Harriet shook her head. 'No,' she said, 'they wouldn't do. It must be Tunbridge Wells, where for the first time in my life I knew a home ... your home, Mamma. Let us go back there together.'

17

Lieutenant Wilberforce might have said truthfully that it was only after his discovery of the contraband at Beauregard Manor that smuggling virtually ceased in the estuary. But he could have said equally that it ceased because Beauregard was sold that September to the Marquis, and presented as a gift to the new Marchioness.

Almost immediately great plans were set on foot for a new Gothic mansion on the site of the old Manor house, the scrubland was cleared and planted with trees, and keepers abounded in the Beauregard woods, where game was to be raised and preserved for the enjoyment of Mr. Sodon and his exalted son-in-law, and the lake was incorporated in a landscape that included the river and its meadowland.

Never had such improvements been seen on such a scale in Beauregard, and most of the villagers, being conservative in their tastes and habits, migrated at length to Cuckford, where there was fish to be found in the bay, and no Mrs. Sodon to force her way into their cottages.

The day after Harriet and her Mamma left the Pells

went too, taking with them what remained of the Beau-regard silver and leaving no address, and soon afterwards Cookson went to live with a married daughter in Wood-rington. Rivers had accompanied Mrs. Tycherley and her step-daughter to Tunbridge Wells.

It was not long before they found a charming house there, quite near Lady Piggott and the Miss Datchetts, who were delighted to welcome them back.

The house had been built at the turn of the century and in consequence was not more than thirty years old, which they felt to be in its favour. It had white stuccoed walls, its windows were large, its rooms spacious, and there were no mullioned windows or low ceilings or dark old panelling to be seen. In fact it was extremely light and airy, and from its windows there were charming views over the town and the common.

Encouraged by Harriet Mrs. Tycherley bought her new furniture, her carpets and her curtains, and while servants were engaged for the house Rivers took charge of the stables, where Molly had Jenny now as a companion to help her in drawing the smart new carriage. Harry Rivers was summoned to become gardener, to his great satisfaction, and Mrs. Tycherley sometimes thought it was as if her nice ordered life there had never been interrupted by Mrs. Slatterly's dreadful lodgings and that horrid old Beauregard.

The only thing that worried her sometimes was that although they appeared to settle down to their new life with the greatest of ease, Harriet's smile had lost a little of its gladness, and there were times, when she thought nobody was taking any notice, that she looked sad. Mrs. Tycherley never mentioned Beauregard, but she wished with all her heart that her step-daughter had not turned her back so resolutely on the friends they had made while they were there.

It was with some delight therefore, if also some inward

trepidation, that she received a letter from Liz Staveley a little while before Christmas. In it she said that she would be visiting friends near Tunbridge Wells on her way to Norfolk to stay with her brother before bringing him back with her to Woodrington for Christmas, and she asked if Harriet had forgiven her sufficiently to receive her if she should call.

Mrs. Tycherley did not show the letter to Harriet, and she wrote off at once begging Liz to come.

I think she misses you and dear Mr. Beauregard more than she will admit, she wrote. *It is unlike Harriet to harbour resentment, and I think her parting words to him have grieved her a great deal, but she is too obstinate to make the first move. But come, dear Liz, and be forgiven. We have never stopped loving you.*

One snowy day in December therefore Mrs. Staveley's carriage stopped at the front door of Mrs. Tycherley's new home and Liz was shown into the drawing-room where Harriet was sitting at work, her Mamma being engaged to play cards that afternoon with Lady Piggott.

For a second Harriet stared as if she could not believe her eyes and then she got up, dropping her work on the floor.

'Why ... Liz!' she exclaimed.

'Dearest Harriet ...' Liz held out her arms. 'Am I forgiven?'

'Oh Liz ... dear, dear Liz!' Harriet was in her arms at once. 'Oh Liz, if you only knew how I have missed you!'

'My dear silly child, why did you not write to me? Or better still, why did you not come and see me before you left Beauregard?'

'I could not ... I was too ashamed ... too humiliated.' Harriet drew back and looked searchingly into her friend's face.

'But why were you ashamed, my dearest child? We were the ones to reproach ourselves, not you! I told Edward that he was only adding to his cousin's cruelty by keeping you in ignorance of what was going on, but he said you were so pleased with that dreadful old house ... and there was no money for you to have proper servants there, or the place fenced in as it should have been.'

'I know ... I have come to realise that.' Harriet drew Liz to the fire and helped her off with her wraps. 'I could not have stopped the smuggling myself. I could not afford even one keeper, let alone the dozen or more that I should have needed to do that. I am sorry, Liz. I misjudged you and Edward. I ought to have known that you would not laugh at me.'

'Laugh at you? But for what, dearest? For being too trusting and innocent? Innocence and trust are too rare qualities to be laughed at by either Edward or myself, I promise you.'

As Harriet knelt down on the floor beside her she took her hand and held it warmly in hers. 'And now let us not talk of Beauregard any more ... tell me what you have been doing here in Tunbridge Wells. This is a charming house ... Are you happy here, Harriet?'

'Mamma loves it all so much,' said Harriet evading the question lightly, 'that I could not fail to find happiness in watching hers.' She withdrew her hand and sat back, her eyes going to the brightly blazing fire. 'All our old friends have been most kind in welcoming us.' She gave a little laugh. 'I am much sought after! Does that surprise you? I can even number Sir Mark Piggott among my suitors!'

'Harriet!' Liz looked down at her affectionately, but as the firelight flickered over her little cousin's face and figure she saw what she had not noticed in the first delight of meeting her again, that she was now very stylishly dressed, her hair hanging in long ringlets that suited her very well, and that her face and figure were thinner. In fact she could see that the little, dumpy charming creature that had won their hearts at Beauregard was gone, and in her place was a much more fashionable and self-possessed young woman, and while she was sorry for it in a way too she was glad. The child at Beauregard had been too vulnerable, too easily hurt. She said gently:

'What is Sir Mark like, Harriet?'

Harriet shrugged her shoulders. 'He is a nice young man, I suppose, but he is dull. He can only talk of a London of which I know nothing: the fashionable districts were never my father's haunts in the old days, and the only parts that I know well are those where the cheaper lodging houses are to be found. Not that I tell him that naturally. It does not do to be too outspoken with people like the Piggotts.' After a moment she went on, 'The country bores Sir Mark, and in fact there is only one thing in his favour, that he does not like killing things. But he is a very good kind of young man, I think, and I daresay he will make an estimable husband.'

Liz was unhappy at the lightness of Harriet's tone. Beauregard had taught her a hard lesson and she had learned it aptly. She said, 'But does he want to marry you then, Harriet?'

'Oh yes. At least, his mother wants him to marry me, and that comes to the same thing, you know.'

'But do you care for him?'

Harriet laughed and scrambled to her feet. 'Does caring matter in a marriage?' she asked. 'Miss Sodon set an example to the young ladies in your part of the world, and no doubt there are many others like her.'

Liz did not reply. She had seen the new Marchioness once only in Woodrington, when she came to call on her old school fellow and stayed exactly ten minutes. She had looked very beautiful and appeared to be extremely happy, her conversation being solely about her husband's grand places and the jewels he had given her.

'Love may not be necessary to the Julia Sodons of this world,' she said at last, 'but it is necessary to you, Harriet. You must not marry without it, my dearest. It would kill you.'

'Ah well, I daresay I shall have plenty to choose from when the time comes.' Harriet's light tone took on an edge. 'Every young man in Tunbridge Wells seems to be anxious for my company since we have returned. Before we left you know I was just "that plain little Miss Tycherley, poor thing," but now I am "the charming, witty and altogether desirable Miss Tycherley." It is wonderful, Liz, what thirty thousand pounds will do to improve a young woman's natural fascination!'

'Now, Harriet, you were never as plain as all that!' Liz was far more grieved than she would reveal, unwilling to lose her little cousin's friendship now that she had regained it. 'So you received thirty thousand pounds for Beauregard?'

'Yes. It was more than the Marquis's man of business wished to give, but I was not in a generous mood.'

Liz was saved from replying by a message brought from her coachman to say that it had started snowing again and it would be advisable not to lose much time in starting out.

'Tell him I am coming at once.' Liz cast an anxious eye at the windows. The sky was yellow and the snow that was falling, though light, showed a determination to continue. She had still another three miles to go over exposed country and she did not wish to get stuck in a drift so that her friends were forced to send out search parties for her.

So she said goodbye regretfully to Harriet and left messages of love for her Mamma, but as the carriage bore her away her thoughts were more on her little cousin than on the journey ahead. 'Oh Harriet,' she thought, 'what did we do to you at Beauregard?'

When she arrived in Norfolk the following week she told her brother of her visit to Tunbridge Wells.

'So Harriet allowed you to see her?' His face lit up. 'Come, that is encouraging! Tell me about her, Liz ... What does she look like? Does she seem to be happy there?'

She told him all she knew and guessed about Harriet. 'She realises now I think that we were not to blame for what happened at Beauregard,' she added. 'But the wound went deep, and she is still suffering from hurt pride. I am afraid she may take some unworthy young man for no other reason than that she can then turn her back on us for ever. And as I am sure that the old Harriet is still there under this coolly assured and rather brittle young lady, I am not happy about her, Edward.'

He shared her concern. 'Liz,' he said anxiously, 'do you think she would see me if I visited her on my way home after Christmas?'

'I daresay she might, but she is in a strange mood. When I tried to stress the unhappiness of a loveless marriage she quoted Julia at me.'

'Julia!' He smiled wryly. He had wasted five years of his life on that young woman and she had not been worth five minutes' thought. Liz was right when she had told him that the only person Miss Sodon had loved had been herself, and it was because of his infatuation for her that he had been blind to what was going on in Beauregard. Liz might not have been to blame for what had happened there, but he could not exonerate himself. He knew the difficulties that Harriet was likely to encounter, and he knew of the danger that threatened her very life in Beauregard, and he had done little to help her or to protect her. It was not due to him in fact that she had escaped being found in the lake.

When Humphrey told him that over five hundred pounds' worth of spirits had been found in the Manor lake, Edward said that he was not surprised.

'Yes. A long, flat-bottomed boat, that they could load up in the valley and bring under the bridge. If they were hard pressed they would put the stuff into the lake, but if not they would take it on upstream as far as the waterfall, where some more of the gang would be waiting with Walter's horses. After that it was an easy matter to take it on up over the scrubland as far as the turnpike.'

'And all this with Walter's knowledge and permission!'

'Oh yes. He made a lot of money out of it. I suspected him for a long time and always prayed that one of his friends might not turn King's Evidence against him. It would have been very embarrassing to have one's wife's cousin before one on a charge of smuggling!'

'They managed to clear the Manor cellars.'

'Yes, mostly in broad daylight I should say.' He laughed at Edward's surprise. 'Old Adam's covered cart would hide a number of casks. He has set himself up in a cooper's business in Woodrington lately.'

Edward smiled. 'So we can say I suppose that smuggling has virtually ceased in Beauregard?'

'Or else that it has moved a little farther on down the coast?' said Humphrey.

All through Christmas among his sister's noisy brood in Woodrington Edward's thoughts were with Harriet and he felt himself to be a dull visitor. It was with a feeling of relief that he set out in the New Year for Tunbridge Wells, posting the thirty miles or so but without much speed because although the snow had gone the roads were hard with frost.

He put up at an hotel in Tunbridge Wells, and after an early dinner he walked round to Mrs. Tycherley's house and found Harriet in the drawing-room, dressed to go out and waiting for her Mamma to join her. When the servant announced him she got up quickly with a small exclamation of pleasure, and gave him her hand, a very self-possessed young lady.

'Edward!' she said. 'How kind of you to come and see us. We had Liz here before Christmas.'

'That is why I am here.' He was grimly amused by her dignity but a little dismayed as well. He had known the old Harriet as well as he had known himself, but this new one he did not know at all. He had to feel his way with her, a new experience that he did not altogether appreciate. After a few exchanges of courtesies and enquiries after Liz and the children on her side, Mrs. Tycherley joined them, full of apologies because they could not offer him dinner, and relieved when he said he had dined.

'We are dining with Lady Piggott,' Harriet said with a slight smile. 'And as Sir Mark is there we have to dine at a fashionable hour. We are very up to date in Tunbridge Wells!'

Mrs. Tycherley asked him to dine with them the following day however and he was pleased to accept. It appeared that they would be alone, as the Piggotts were engaged elsewhere.

'We see a great deal of them,' Harriet's Mamma said with a fond look at her that spoke volumes. He glanced at his cousin with more attention and noticed for the first time that her finery eclipsed that of Beauregard, and he regretted the green dress of contraband silk and the green ribbon that had been threaded in her hair. He could not think that Mark Piggott, even if he were a baronet, was worth the time and trouble that had been spent on her appearance that evening.

He spent a restless night on the uncomfortable hotel bed and the following morning, after a brisk walk over the Common, he decided not to wait for the evening before calling on Harriet again. As he drew near the house however he met young Harry Rivers setting out for the Library with a bundle of books tucked under his arm. He recognised Edward at once with a delighted grin.

'Mr. Beauregard!' he cried, touching his hat. 'I didn't know as you was here in Tunbridge Wells.'

Edward explained that he was on a short visit to the town after spending Christmas in Woodrington.

'I heard one bit of good news while I was there,' he added. 'That fellow Jake has been caught and given transportation for life. I feel that all of us who have Beauregard blood in our veins may now sleep the better for it.'

'Aye, I'm glad on Miss Harriet's account for sure,' said young Harry. 'It was a near thing that night, sir, down in that there Gazebo.'

'I know that, Harry.' Edward's face was grave. 'Did you ever discover who the other man was?'

'Why no, sir, not exactly . . . But it may have been Dawlish.'

'Dawlish eh . . .? You are probably right. He was a good-hearted rascal, that old fellow.'

'I did hear a rumour as he was giving up the Lobster Pot and taking the Harbour Light in Cuckford,' went on Harry with the suspicion of a wink, and Edward said he thought that was probably true as well.

He walked on to Mrs. Tycherley's house and found the widow there alone. Sir Mark, she explained, had taken Harriet out driving in his carriage that morning.

'I do not mind Sir Mark taking her,' she went on. 'He is such a careful driver—unlike some of the other young gentlemen in Tunbridge Wells. They cut the corners and drive like the wind, Mr. Beauregard, almost as if the next moment must be their last.'

Edward felt annoyed and irritated with Sir Mark Piggott. What right had he to go taking Harriet out when he wanted to talk to her himself? Mrs. Tycherley did not improve his temper either by her archness whenever she mentioned Sir Mark and Harriet in the same breath, and at last he felt forced to take himself off for another walk over the Common to relieve his feelings.

It was only as he was returning to his hotel that his irritation left him: he saw Harriet coming to look for him.

'I am so glad I have found you, Edward,' she said at once in a way that banished his ill-temper, so like it was to the sweetness of the old Harriet in Beauregard. 'I am afraid I am in need of your advice again.' She smiled at him uncertainly. 'I came to you so often in Beauregard, you know, and you never failed me.'

'On the contrary I am afraid that I did fail you ... often,' he said. He gave her his arm and turned back with her. 'Tell me how I can help you.'

'It is about Sir Mark Piggott,' she said. 'He has not made me an offer yet, but every time he comes to the house or we go to his mother's I can see it trembling on his lips, and I have to use all my wits not to be left alone with him. Last night it was a near thing. His mother asked him to show me the plants in the conservatory, but luckily there was a deaf aunt there and I asked her to come and tell us the names of the plants, which she did with the greatest pleasure. And then this morning of course there was the groom sitting up behind, and I kept our conversation entirely to the horses. I never thought I'd be able to find so much to say about horses in the whole of my life!' She sighed. 'But I know I cannot put it off much longer. It is becoming almost worse than avoiding Mr. Wilberforce.'

'If I remember correctly you had no trouble in refusing the Lieutenant's offer.' Edward's voice was dry, and she shook his arm impatiently in the old way—a way that delighted him by its warm intimacy.

'Oh do not be so tiresome, Edward! Of course I can refuse Sir Mark, but if I do it will ruin Mamma's friendship with Lady Piggott, and she dotes on it—she always has. And if I marry him Mamma will not have the means to live here in her lovely new house.'

'Has she no money of her own then?'

'Not a sixpence. My father robbed her of all she had, home, friends and money. It is the Beauregard property that has paid for everything here, and I am happy beyond words that it should be so.'

'Then where is the difficulty?'

'Why, don't you see if I marry Sir Mark he will expect to have the control of my income—he would not dream of proposing marriage if he did not. And to rob my dear Mamma a second time will break my heart and hers.'

He wondered if she had ever considered herself except for those disastrous months at Beauregard as he said gently, 'But my dear child, all this can be arranged. There are such things as marriage settlements, by which Mrs. Tycherley could be assured of an adequate income, if this is what you wish. I am sure Sir Mark will not be unreasonable over that. But if a marriage is not founded on love, my dear, it is worthless. Do you love young Piggott, Harriet?'

She replied as she had to Liz. 'He is a good sort of young man.' But he could see she was distressed. 'Oh Edward, what does it matter beside Mamma's happiness?'

'It matters more than her happiness, more than her friendship for Lady Piggott.'

'I daresay I might come to have affection for him in time.' Harriet's voice was bleak. 'There seems to be no way out of it, does there, Edward? I shall have to marry him.'

He did not reply for a long moment and then he said, 'There is one way out, if we leave your own inclinations out of it, as you seem determined to do. There is a way in which your Mamma can live on here tranquilly in the full enjoyment of her house and her friends.'

'What is that?' She waited hopefully. 'Dear Edward, I knew you would think of something. You always do.'

. 'Don't let your hopes soar too high.' The smile he gave her was strained, and had a touch of mockery in it, though whether he was mocking himself or her she did not know. 'I know I am old for you, child, but I've enough money of my own never to want a penny of yours. Your Mamma would be welcome to it until she died, and in the meantime if she could tell her friend Lady Piggott, that you were engaged to be married to your cousin, I do not think there could be any offended dignity or hurt feelings anywhere. In fact it should be a matter of congratulation all round.'

She looked as if she did not know whether to laugh or to cry, whether to be proud or humbled. 'I conclude that you are making me an offer, Edward,' she said uncertainly.

'I *am* making you an offer, Harriet.' But his voice was not as steady as he would have wished. What was he doing, he wondered? Had he gone mad? And yet he could see little Harriet in his house in Norfolk as he had never seen Julia there ... Little Harriet, singing in the rooms as she sang at Beauregard, out of tune and yet so happily ... Little Harriet turning in her saddle to laugh at him, asking his advice, teasing him, coming to him for everything, trusting him, giving him warmth and companionship, and if he dare hope for it, love. 'It would be more convenient for you,' he said evenly.

'Convenient?' Her wide mouth trembled. 'You have a very unromantic way of puttings things, Edward.'

'I am not a very romantic sort of man. If you want romance you'd better stick to Piggott.' He was so offended that it was all she could do to keep from laughing.

'*He* isn't romantic either,' she said. 'In fact, I am afraid he is finding the thought of getting married a most dreadful bore ... Would you find it a bore, Edward?'

'A bore? With you?' Their eyes met and suddenly he laughed. 'I could shake you for teasing me!' he cried. 'Of all the exasperating creatures ... But I suppose that is why I love you, Harriet, and why ... I shall be the happiest man on earth if you will marry me.'

'Oh Edward!' She clasped her free hand with the other, locking them through his arm. 'Why have you been away from me so long? I have missed you so much ...'

'You said you never wanted to see me again,' he reminded her, but his hand closed on hers, warm and strong.

'I know I did, but I was so stupid and hurt, and I wanted to hurt others ... and especially those I loved best. Oh Edward, my dearest dear, please never let me lose you again!'

* * *

They were married that February, and it was not until the following May that Sir Mark Piggott forgot Harriet in the pursuit of another young lady, this time with thirty-five thousand pounds of her own. Owing to the efforts of his mother and the lady concerned he was successful in winning her, and Mrs. Tycherley was able to write to Harriet in her new home to tell her of the engagement, and that the marriage had been arranged for the end of July.

In the meantime however the interest of the event was overshadowed by the death of the King. Lady Piggott received a first hand account of it from her son, and after he had returned to London she summoned Mrs. Tycherley and the Miss Datchetts to hear the details of how the Archbishop and Lord Clarendon had arrived at six o'clock in the morning at Kensington Palace to arouse the young Queen.

It was a beautiful June day and Mrs. Tycherley put on her favourite dress for the occasion, remembering how Lady Piggott had admired it when she wore it before. In fact she had been kind enough to say that she had never seen her old friend in a more beautiful dress, or in one that became her better, and Mrs. Tycherley had admitted that she had not worn it while Harriet was with her because she did not like it. 'In fact,' she had added with a touch of guilt, 'she does not know that I still have it.'

But the occasion was worthy of the dress and as she sipped her tea and listened to Lady Piggott she felt almost as if she had been in the Palace herself at the time.

'Fancy a Queen of England again!' said the elder Miss Datchett shaking her head disapprovingly.

'With *that* ancestry too!' added her sister.

'She is a year younger than Harriet,' said Mrs. Tycherley moist-eyed. 'Dear girl! It seems only yesterday that she was a tiny child riding her little donkey over our Commons, bless her.'

The elder Miss Datchett said it was a pity the Hanovers were so plain.

'In my son's opinion,' said Lady Piggott severely, 'we may be starting on a new era, an era of prosperity and respectability. Yes, that is what he said to me this morning before he started out for London. "Depend on it, Mamma," he said, "it is not a bad thing for a nation as great as ours to have a sovereign straight from the schoolroom." And then he said—I hope I won't shock you, but you know what gentlemen are over these things!—"It is a great deal more respectable," he said "to come from a governess to a throne than from a mistress." '

Mrs. Tycherley did not know why her thoughts went at that moment to Beauregard, which had not been at all respectable. Parcels of land ... parcels of silk and lace ... those poor dear men, went her confused thoughts, meaning so well ... although it was all so wrong, of course ... and filling the lake with their brandy ... 'Respectability,' she echoed, smoothing the grey silk and its lovely French lace with tender fingers, 'yes, I am sure Sir Mark is right ... It is a quality that has been too little esteemed in our dear country of late.'

Parcels of silk ... and parcels of lace ... She smiled demurely over her tea-cup. 'There is undoubtedly a great deal to be said in its favour,' she said.

THE AMATEUR GOVER[

MARY ANN GIBBS

All the bells of London were ringing in
the Queen's Diamond Jubilee and the
New Year Ball, Catherine Whittingham
ceiving a passionate proposal from he
son.

But the night which should have b
happiest of Catherine's life was to be bligh
tragedy which left her not only bereft of
but, to her astonishment, utterly penniless
To accept marriage now would seem littl
than begging and instead, she realised, the
ceivable was now a necessity — she must a
find employment to support herself and her
young sister, Bella.

With her pampered and wealthy chil
consigned to the past Catherine found h
with only her courage and ingenuity to hel
in a different world, at the mercy of her st
employers and for the first time in her life,
pletely alone.

CORONET BOOKS